THREE PUNCH COMBO

PAUL BISHOP

WOLFPACK
PUBLISHING
— EST 2013 —

Published in the United States by Wolfpack Publishing, Las Vegas

Wolfpack Publishing
6032 Wheat Penny Avenue
Las Vegas, NV 89122

wolfpackpublishing.com

Paperback ISBN 978-1-64119-925-4
eBook ISBN 978-1-64119-826-4

THREE PUNCH COMBO

CONTENTS

I. FIGHTCARD: FELONY FISTS

ROUND ONE

I was leaning back against the ring ropes, elbows tucked in, arms up, gloves protecting my face and head. Lester *Killer* Carter was banging away at me, thinking he could finish the fight fast, and I was letting him. Not because I didn't have a choice, but because I had a plan.

It was still early, and the Los Angeles Olympic Auditorium was less than a quarter full. My fight with Carter wasn't even listed on the night's card, just a middleweight amateur three-round bout to get the evening rolling.

However, Mickey Cohen, a squat toad of a man, was there ringside. His bodyguards sat behind him, while on either side, there were a couple of expensive looking ring Jezebels—the kind of women who liked to get a man's blood splattered across their dresses. Sitting stoically next to the woman on Cohen's left was the huge black bulk of Solomon King, the man who was Cohen's current light-heavyweight contender.

Word was, King was the real deal. His tall frame was packed with massive muscles. Long arms were capped by fourteen-inch fists, which King used to club his opponents relentlessly. Boxing reporters speculated Cohen had King on track to fight Archie Moore, the current light-heavyweight champion, later in the year. But King would have to decisively win at least one more fight, against a viable contender before Moore's people would allow the championship belt to be put on the line. King was the kind of fighter champions dodged for as long as they could.

I shot out a left jab, rocking Carter's head back. It was just hard enough to make him mad. Carter started swinging wildly, and I went back into my defensive shell.

Cohen had a lot of much more lucrative, if illicit, businesses, but he loved the fights. Carter was reputed to be headed into Cohen's stable, but I was going to make sure the big man was disappointed in this particular prospect.

I rolled off the ropes and scooted away to Carter's left. He followed throwing a right cross, which I batted easily away. He should have thrown a left to drive me back to the ropes, but Carter didn't have a left worth writing home about. I let him chase me for a bit and then stopped and threw a triple combination designed to sting, but not hurt. All three punches scored, drawing more embarrassment for Carter than pain.

The bell rang to end the first round, and I swayed back to avoid Carter's late left hook. It went past me like a weak breeze. The ref, a short fat man in black pants, white shirt, and red bow tie, jumped between us.

In my corner, Pop Hawks was waiting with my stool. Before I sat, I looked directly at Cohen. Catching his eye, I pumped my left arm up and down in a mocking motion, rubbing in his fighter's weakness. I didn't like Cohen. Most cops didn't unless they were on his payroll.

That Cohen shared a first name with my older brother was a disgrace.

Cohen had filled the organized crime void in L.A. in '47 when mobster Bugsy Siegel ate a bullet sandwich in his home because he wouldn't play ball with the east coast crime families. While Cohen did pay token respect to the east, he was tougher and more violent than Bugsy ever dreamed of being. Most everyone, made-men included, gave him a wide berth.

"What are you doing out there?" Pops growled, taking out my mouthpiece and tipping water in my mouth before I could answer. I was slick with sweat but felt instantly cooled when Tina Hawks, Pops' thirteen-year-old daughter, squeezed a sponge across my shoulders. She then held a bucket for me to spit in. Growing up around a family full of older brothers, Tina was a tomboy and a half. Tall and skinny now, she'd be a beauty someday, but she wouldn't want to hear about it now.

"Easy, Pops," I said. "He's punching himself out, and I'm not even breathing heavy."

"Don't mess around in a fight. He could lucky punch you, then you're on your back being counted out."

Ex-navy swab, Pops Hawks had left the Los Angeles Police Department after eight years and a bullet in his leg to run Ten Hawks Gym—named for him and his nine kids. All the Hawks were fighters either in the ring or out.

Pops had the cauliflowered ears and eye scarring of a palooka, but he still had his brains if not his looks. Ten Hawks Gym was just down the street from Central Division Station, where I was assigned to the night watch felony car. Pops coddled part-time fighters like me and dreamed of training a contender.

I looked over at Cohen and his following again. The gangster was chatting away, but Solomon King wasn't paying any attention. He was staring straight at me. His eyes were dead pools of hate. I'd seen that look before from other Negros I'd been with in the Navy. It was a look of them against the world. King's burned harder.

I noticed another large negro sitting behind King. He was perhaps an inch shorter but had the same ebony carved expression. A comma of straight, short, white hair stuck out on the left side of his forehead, stark against the wiry curls of his otherwise tar black hair.

"Who's sitting behind King?" I asked Pops.

He didn't even turn to look. "Focus, Flynn. Get out there and put this guy down."

The bell sounded. I popped up off the stool and into a barrage of punches. Carter had obviously been fired up in his corner. He knew Cohen was watching, and he wanted to look good. As long as he was progressing, Cohen would fund his rise. One setback and Cohen would lose interest.

I backed into the ropes, rolling easily with one of Carter's right hooks. Out of the corner of my eye, I caught one of the women with Cohen, the redhead, watching me intently. For a second, I thought I recognized her, but then I had to get busy fending off Carter.

I wrapped Carter in a clinch. Over his shoulder, I could see Cohen was watching, waving his arms around and getting animated.

King just watched.

I let Carter push me away and went back to work counterpunching.

I knew a lot about Cohen. When he was a teenager, he began boxing in illegal prizefights in Los Angeles. In 1930 he turned pro against Patsy Farr in Cleveland, Ohio. He'd been a pretty good featherweight. He even had a shot in '31 against World Featherweight Champion Tommy Paul. In that real fight, he hadn't lasted long. Paul knocked out Gangster Mickey Cohen, as he was known even then, at 2:20 into the first round.

Cohen's last fight in the ring was in '33, twenty-one years ago, against Baby Arizmendi in Tijuana, Mexico. It was another beat down. Now, he fought in the streets where there were no rules, using guns and blades and other men as deadly punches to climb another type of championship ladder. Cohen was a heavyweight, out of my league as a beat cop, but it didn't mean I couldn't take down one of his puppets.

I fended off a couple more strong rights from Carter and then walked into a weak left hook—only it wasn't. It was fast and hit with the force of a boulder. I staggered and reeled away, suckered like some tin can just waiting to be knocked over. Carter followed relentlessly, throwing combinations I couldn't answer. I hated being a sucker. My brother Mickey would have razzed me. He always said I didn't take fighting serious enough.

I clinched, wrapping my arms around Carter, burying my head in his shoulder. He tried to push me away, but I held him tight like I'd paid a dime for the dance.

The ref tapped me on the shoulder and yelled, "Break!"

My head had cleared a little and I covered up as I pulled away. Carter threw another of those sucker lefts, but I was ready for it. I slipped it and stepped in to throw a couple of weak jabs. They didn't do much damage and Carter came back at me again.

I clinched again and was still waltzing with him when the bell rang.

"Stupid!" Pops said as I sat on the stool. "I taught ya better..."

I was waiting for Tina to sponge my back, but instead she popped up next to Pops and handed him a folded piece of paper. Pops knew Tina didn't fool around, so he took her serious and opened it.

"Where'd this come from?"

"The negro with the white in his hair handed it to me."

Pops turned the paper toward me.

It read—On The Canvas This Round

There was only one source that cared enough to get me to throw a fight. There wasn't any threat attached. There didn't have to be. I looked over, and the Negro man with the white comma of hair was back sitting behind Cohen and King. Messenger boy.

"What you going to do, Pat?" Tina asked.

"I don't go in the tank for nobody," I said, standing up.

I couldn't believe Cohen cared much about a small-time amateur fight, but I cared. With the Navy, I'd been assigned to the battleship Missouri in the Eastern Med when Truman was rattling his Cold War saber. I'd boxed on the deck for the Navy and on shore leave for the honor of the ship, and I wasn't going down for some two-bit gangster no matter who he was.

The bell rang, and I came out of the corner on fire. In the Navy, I fought whoever they put in front of me. The sanctioned fights had kept to official weight standards when they could, but on shore, in the bars and behind fuel dumps, I'd never walked away from bigger, heavier men. I'd taken my lumps, but I'd developed a reputation for being a giant killer. I was a David taking on Goliaths with just my fists, no sling needed.

There had been some split decisions along the way, even a couple of bad beatings, but I'd never gone down for the count. Not once.

I boxed these days simply because I'd always boxed. Between the nuns and Father Tim at St. Vincent's Asylum for Boys in Chicago, where Mickey and I grew up, I'd been made tougher than an old elephant's hide.

We'd called the asylum Our Lady of the Glass Jaw, simply because the nuns hated the nickname. They made us pay for it regularly. Their pious anger and Father Tim's fast hands in the ring challenging us were what made us tough and proud.

I kept in shape now and fought regularly, but without a goal. I wasn't hungry, but I still hadn't gone down for the count, and I wasn't going to start now.

Carter saw me coming. He knew instantly something was different. I was Patrick Felony Flynn. I was a giant killer, and I saw the fear in his eyes. I hated that fear because it was the fear of weak bullies.

I feinted with my left and sent a right straight from my shoulder, blowing between Carter's raised fists. His head snapped back, but this time there was more behind the punch than the last time I'd tagged him.

Then I went for Carter's exposed body. I was seeing red. On some level, I was aware of the small crowd starting to pay attention. I didn't just want to stop Carter; I wanted to destroy him. It was as if by destroying him, I could destroy Cohen. Stupid thinking.

Carter had a good core, but not a great one. There were a lot of miles not run, a lot of sit-ups not done, and I made him pay for his laxity. My gloves pounded at his gut as I ignored the off-balance punches he threw.

When Carter's hands dropped, I drove through them with an uppercut hitting him on the button. He was going down, but I propped him against the ropes and let loose. I was lost inside myself. The unreasoning anger I'd always known since I was a child was hot and raging. I hit him again and again until the ref and Pops pulled me back.

Carter dropped. Done. Finished. If he ever got in the ring again, he'd end up the same way. I saw the fear in him and knew I'd broken him for boxing.

I pulled away from Pops, spitting out my mouth-piece. I walked over to the ropes and looked down at Cohen. I spat a gob of blood on the canvas in contempt.

If anything, Cohen looked amused. He clapped his hands slowly, puffing on the cigar stuck in the middle of his mouth. The redhead next to him looked uncomfortable. Somehow, she didn't seem a match with the blonde on Cohen's right. She was dressed in the same floozy glamour, a too tight dress and gaudy jewelry, but there was intelligence in her eyes saying she didn't belong there.

The Negro guy with the white comma of hair was gone, but King was there. He was sitting motionless, giving me his hard, flat stare.

I wasn't worried about him. He was a pro and I was an amateur. He was a light-heavyweight; I'd always fought as a middleweight. The only way I'd ever come face to face with him was in a back alley, and then I'd have the good sense to run.

Pops and Tina threw my robe over me and guided me to the center of the ring where the ref raised my hand for half a second and let it drop. This was nothing to him. A small fight in a big venue. Not even on the card.

ROUND TWO

Two days after the Carter bout, I was back in blue with a badge pinned to my chest. I was assigned to L.A.P.D.'s Central Division felony prowl car. Even though it was still a uniformed assignment, the felony car didn't respond to routine calls, instead being free to hunt down burglars, robbers, and ex-cons who hadn't taken to the rehabilitation offered in prison.

My regular partner, Bump Smith, had called in sick, so I was cruising by myself. I preferred things this way. Bump was assigned to the felony car because he was the senior uniform on the watch, but senior didn't equate to efficient. He was a fat, greedy, chain-smoking racist, who used his badge as an excuse to bully drunks, beggars, Negroes, and Hispanics. He didn't like me, and I didn't like him, but he had fifteen years on the job to my three. He never took kickbacks when I was around, but I knew he was dirty, and it caused friction.

Without Bump to slow me down, I'd already booked a warrant suspect I'd spotted casing a small family market, pulled a gun off a gambler outside Union Train Station, and worked my street informants for an ex-con pulling roof jobs on local drug stores.

It was getting on toward midnight, and the downtown streets were relatively quiet. The area was mostly businesses with some flophouses and low-end residences thrown in. Most of the smaller businesses had living quarters up above. The nighttime population was mostly Negro and Hispanic or troublemakers – people looking for happy powder or happy girls. If you were white, and not just passing through, then you were on skid row and nobody cared.

It would be another two hours before the drunks left the bars, but they were somebody else's problem.

Even when I'd been working a regular patrol car, I'd always gone after the high-end arrests. There were plenty of blue uniformed thugs who didn't want to do anything more than harass streetwalkers, stumblebums, and petty thieves, and if they were Mexican or Negro, all the better. It was safe work, throwing their weight around and hiding behind their badges, but it wasn't for me.

I wanted out of the blue monkey suit and into plain clothes. There were still detectives with the same mentality as the uniformed thugs, but there were chances to get away from them and make a difference.

I'd recently taken the promotional test to make detective. Since I didn't have a lot of time on the job, I needed to make sure my arrest record sparkled when it came time for the interview part of the promotion process.

I'd had enough of uniforms in the Navy to last me a lifetime. I wanted to do something more than just go where I was ordered. In the Navy, it meant being ordered to stay in the ring and out of the action. The Navy Boxing Team had held up the honor of the seas against all comers, be they Marines, Army, or the pretty boys from the Air Force who could fly like the devil but couldn't punch their way out of a pillowcase.

As soon as the Navy found out I had an iron jaw and knew what to do with my fists, they kept me out of regular duty, but I was itching to get a crack at the Commies from the firing line. But even the firing line in the Eastern Mediterranean was all bluff and bluster. The *Missouri* was willing and ready, but the Soviets just lay sleeping.

It was all well and good eating steak, skipping rope, and sparring, but I wanted more. I wanted to be where the action was. I tried everything. I got off the *Missouri* and onto a gunboat going up the Yangzi, but none of the Communist Chinese wanted to take on the might of the U.S. Navy – the Sleeping Dragon stayed sleeping.

I even volunteered for the Shore Patrol, but it was worse – every dive and bar I went in to, my brother Mickey and his flying fists had been there before. Everyone knew him, and they thought they'd have their revenge on me. I started more fights than I broke up.

After four years of fighting American servicemen instead of the enemy, I'd had enough. I mustered out in San Diego in '49. And wouldn't you know, it was a year too soon—1950 saw the North Korean Commies going south and a real war was on. They called it a conflict or a police action, but you try and explain the difference to the boys struggling to keep one hill and take the next.

Mickey, in the Merchant Marine now, had been there among them. I'd almost reenlisted, but the recruiter pulled my record, and I would have gone right back to fighting in the ring instead of the front. I wanted more.

With Father Tim turning a blind eye, because he figured it was for the best, I'd lied about my age and joined the Navy at fifteen. After I was discharged, it wasn't hard to keep those extra fake years and put them on the L.A.P.D. application to say I was twenty-one.

Three years later, it didn't seem to matter much. Everybody on the L.A.P.D. started in uniform after graduating from the police academy, but I was determined to go further. I was working hard, making good arrests, and developing a reputation as Felony Flynn. I was just hoping it would be enough to get me promoted.

Chief Parker was trying to clean up the department, getting rid of slugs like Bump and separating the cops from the crooks. His personal rough riders were known as The Hat Squad, a group of hand-picked detectives working directly for the chief. Their official title was The Gangster Squad, but their sharp suits and fedoras gave them The Hat Squad nickname.

The Hat Squad took on all the goons and thugs who worked for guys like Mickey Cohen. Getting the mob's big boys was almost impossible, but taking out levels of their organization and making them feel the heat was what The Hat Squad specialized in. They were really something, and I wanted to be part of that something. I hated the feeling I had at the Olympic, knowing there was nothing I could do to a guy like Cohen.

My show of bravado hadn't meant anything other than letting Cohen mark my card. The department was still full of guys like Bump who were in Cohen's pocket. Parker was weeding them out, but they could still make trouble for a guy like me.

I realized I wasn't paying proper attention when a new model Cadillac blew out of an alley onto Main Street right in front of me. I slammed on the brakes and pulled the wheel to the left. The Caddy fishtailed, just slipping around me, and sped away. I caught a glimpse of a young couple scared out of their wits in the front seat.

The car, the couple, their clothes, the look on their faces, all clicked through my brain in a split second. They weren't the problem. I knew what a couple of rich kids in one of their daddies' cars had been doing in the alley in this part of town—looking for cheap thrills buying reefer. I didn't care about them, but something had scared them, and the bigger bust was probably still down the alley.

I got the prowl car stopped before it crossed the alley mouth. I pushed open the door and slid out, pulling on my sap gloves and grabbing my hickory nightstick. Sap gloves worked like a charm. There were pads of sand sewn into the palms and along the backs of the fingers. You could slap a man down and ring his bell without ever making a fist.

I reached back into the car and grabbed the radio mike from its hook on the dash. "One F Eighteen, officer needs back-up, north-south alley west of Main and Third." Most of the other night watch units would be circling the station waiting to go *end of watch*, but the back-up call would get them rolling my way.

"One F Eighteen, roger," the female voice of the RTO, radio telephone operator, responded and then put out the call over the main frequency.

I crouched down and peeked around into the alley. What I saw brought me immediately to my feet and sprinting toward trouble.

In the spillover light from a streetlamp, I could see three figures beating on a fourth who had just fallen to the ground. The standing figures were wielding lengths of pipe and intended on doing some serious damage.

I had a .38 on my hip, but I didn't need it. Being outnumbered didn't bother me. Mickey and I had always been outnumbered.

I didn't call out, and the standing trio didn't hear me coming. They thought they had it all their way and were taking their time salivating over their victim like a pack of wild dogs.

I saw a lead pipe come up, ready to swing down on the legs of the man on the ground. I swung my nightstick—two and a half feet of hardwood—and broke the hand holding the pipe.

The owner of the hand yelped like a little girl, dropping the pipe and sticking his injured mitt between his knees. I clouted him hard over one ear with the open, sand-filled, palm of my free hand and he went down without a peep. All of a sudden, the odds had changed from three on one to two on two, even though the Negro kid who was getting the beating was still on the ground with his knees pulled up and his arms over this head.

"Hello, boys," I said with a wicked smile. "What's this all about?"

The shock of my appearance on the scene froze the action for a second. Both of the remaining thugs were ten or more years older than the kid on the ground and both were white. I recognized one of them as a low-level soldier from Cohen's mob named Tellis. The guy with him was taller and skinnier, with a pock-marked face and a honker the size of a schooner. I'd seen his face on a wanted poster for assault. His name was Cooper.

"You don't want none of this, Flynn," Tellis said.

"Is that so?" I was just close enough to throw out a jab with my nightstick. It caught Tellis in the gut and he doubled over.

Cooper jumped forward, swinging his length of lead pipe at me. As he did, he had to step over the kid on the ground. The kid suddenly came to life, kicking upward into Cooper's exposed groin—hard. Cooper reacted as you would expect, the pain causing him to stumble over the kid and fall to the ground.

I was surprised. The kid had sand. As Cooper fell, it was no sweat for me to step him and sap glove him the rest of the way to the ground.

Tellis had backed away from me and straightened up. I'd only given him a love tap, and he'd recovered quickly.

"He's cutting in on our turf," Tellis said, pointing at the kid. "He had to be taught a lesson."

"This isn't your turf." Sirens shrilled and closed in on us, getting closer by the second.

Tellis had a reputation as a hard man. He wasn't going to go quietly.

He came at me swinging his pipe at my head.

Street fighting was a lot different than fighting in the ring. In street fighting, there was only one rule – win.

I blocked the swinging pipe with my nightstick, then whipped the hickory down onto the juncture where Tellis' neck met his shoulder.

Tellis howled and dropped his pipe. I pulled the nightstick back and swung it again, this time lower and harder—taking out Tellis' knee. He fell to the ground yowling and curled into a ball.

The Negro kid had scrambled to his feet, but he hadn't gone anywhere. He was just standing and trembling. He couldn't have been more than thirteen or fourteen.

A prowl car with siren blaring and lights blazing pulled into the far end of the alley and raced toward us. Another entered on the near end. The cavalry was arriving almost too soon.

"Where's the dope, kid?" I asked.

"What..." He may have had sand, but a lot of it was between his ears at the moment.

"The reefer!"

"He took it," he said, pointing to the first guy I took down.

The two prowl cars screeched to a halt and uniforms poured out. Guns and nightsticks were everywhere. The kid threw his hands up in the air. Telis and Cooper were still groaning on the ground. The first one I'd hit with the sap gloves was still out.

"Easy," I said loudly to the arriving cops. "It's under control."

Evans, the watch sergeant, stepped up next to me. He looked around at the human debris on the ground. "What's going on, Felony? Don't look like you need any back-up."

"Just a hand running these goons in."

"Charge?" Evan's asked.

"Filth and ignorance in the presence of a police officer." It was an old line, but Evans still chuckled. Other cops were putting handcuffs on the three thugs. The Negro kid was still standing there with his hands up, but everyone was ignoring him.

"They were drunk and disorderly," I said. "If you search the one over there, you'll probably find enough to book him for a felony." I indicated the thug who had taken the dope from the Negro kid. "I recognize the tall one from a wanted flyer. You can let the other go after he's sobered up."

"You're not taking the felony bust?"

"Not tonight. I already got my quota."

"What about Sambo?" Evans asked, tilting his chin to indicate the Negro kid.

"Uninvolved witness," I said. "Wrong place, wrong time."

"I'm sure we can find some charge to fit," Evans said. He was a casual racist—the worst kind. Every Negro person was Sambo to him, man or woman. He was like my partner, Bump, stupid and lazy.

"Be satisfied with the trio," I said.

Evans nodded. It was nothing to him.

I knew the three men would keep their mouths shut about the real situation. They weren't drunk, but that was a negligible detail. Sergeant Evans wouldn't push the point. He knew how the game was played.

The other cops had the three thugs on their feet and headed toward the prowl cars. Evans nodded to me again, then walked away to follow them.

I reached over and grabbed the Negro kid by the scruff of his collar. "What's your name."

"R...Ro...Rodney," he stuttered. "Rodney Stone."

"Relax, Rodney," I said. "How old are you?"

"Eighteen."

I laughed, pulling his collar tight and pushing my face into his. "Lie to me again and I'll call Sergeant Evans back. I'm sure he can find room in the Gray Bar Hotel for you with the others." I shook him. "Now, how old are you?"

"Fourteen, sir...Fourteen." He was trembling again.

"Where are your parents?"

"Don't got no daddy. Momma died last week."

On paper, my story was the reverse. In reality, it was a lot worse. Mickey and I were alone on the Chicago streets when I was eight and he was ten. The orphanage was a nightmare, except for Father Tim. The priest was the biggest, meanest, fairest, most loving man I've ever known. Everything I know about fighting, boxing, and being a man, I owed to him.

"Come on." I gave Rodney a shove in the direction of the alley mouth where my prowl car was parked. He scampered ahead of me, but I still had my hand on his collar. He wasn't going anywhere I didn't want him to go.

"Who gave you the dope to sell? I asked.

Rodney was too scared not to answer. "Mr. Hudson. He's gonna kill me."

Amos Hudson ran the Negro gangs in the city. His skin was a different color, but he was just as bad as Mickey Cohen. Vice wasn't racist; it debased and humiliated everyone.

"You aren't going to have to worry about Hudson," I said. At the prowl car, I opened the passenger door and shoved Rodney in.

"Where you takin' me?"

"Bonnie Wallace's."

Bonnie ran a Negro brothel. She also had a soft spot for kids. She'd give Rodney a bed. Using my money, she'd call ahead to Father Tim and let him know I was sending him another orphan, and then she'd get Rodney on a bus to Chicago. If he stayed on the bus all the way, Father Tim would take him in and teach him to survive – just like he'd taught me and Mickey.

Mickey and I both sent money fairly regularly. Every once in a while, I'd send a kid. Rodney had shown he had sand in the alley when he kicked Cooper. He was on the wrong path—the same one Mickey and I had been on. If he took it, Father Tim would give him a chance.

As I got in the prowl car on the driver's side, I looked across the street and saw a plainclothes detective sedan parked at the curb. A big Negro man in a sharp dark suit leaned against the front fender. The fedora on his head was pushed back, and I could see the tuft of white in his hair.

I looked at him. He looked at me.

There was no doubt he was a cop—a detective. There weren't many Negro cops on the force, but there were a few in patrol. I didn't know of any Negro detectives. The hat, the suit, and the flashy detective sedan put him way above the station where men like him were usually forced to stay.

He was wearing the signature fedora of the Hat Squad, Chief Parker's elite gangster squad.

Yet I knew he was in Gangster Mickey Cohen's pocket.

ROUND THREE

As far as I could tell, there hadn't been any fallout from the arrests the night before. I hadn't expected any. Even though we were supposed to be the good guys, we boys in blue were the toughest gang in town. We took care of our own. I had no doubt Cohen's flunkies would carry word back to him about the events and my intervention.

To save their own skins with Cohen, they would have to make up a good reason for why three of them couldn't handle one kid and a cop. The version Cohen heard would make it sound as if they had been set up by all the cops who had finally arrived.

Since Tellis knew me, I figured my name would come up on Cohen's radar again. I wasn't sure if I wanted the notoriety. It wasn't healthy to keep coming to a mob boss' attention. If Cohen thought I was running a campaign against him, I might soon be dodging bullets instead of fists. However, I figured I was low level enough not to make Cohen go out of his way to do something about me.

I also figured it wouldn't hurt my chances of promotion to be seen as somebody who wasn't scared to do his job, even if it meant taking on connected thugs.

Midway through the following morning, I was at Ten Hawks Gym watching Billy Two-Shoes let a young Mexican kid, named Chico, tag him with an ambitious, but weak three punch combination.

The gym was always filled with shadows due to the grimy windows and bad ceiling lighting. There was little ventilation to reduce the smell of sweat, leather, liniment, and testosterone. The walls were plastered with posters from old fights slapped up between old mirrors. However, despite hard use, Pops managed to keep the three rings in decent shape along with the rest of the equipment.

"Faster," Pops said from ringside.

Chico threw the left jab, right jab, left uppercut again with no appreciable difference.

"What are you, on siesta? Harder! Faster!" Pops said, and Chico let fly again. This time Billy swatted away the punches. He then stepped in and threw two lightning jabs, each barely touching the tip of Chico's nose inside his headgear.

"Enough!" Pops called out, and Billy floated away. Billy was sixteen going on thirty. Chico was barely ten. Billy was on his way to the Golden Gloves. Chico was just trying to make it through another Saturday.

Pops pulled himself into the ring and started showing Billy a new combination to take advantage of his fast hands.

I set a stool down in the opposite corner. Chico flopped down on it. There were tears of frustration in his eyes, but he wouldn't let them fall.

"You did good," I told him.

"Pops say too slow..." Chico tailed off. His English was bad enough without his mouthpiece in place. The red gloves on his fists looked huge at the ends of his stringy arms. I was surprised he could even hold them up, let alone throw punches.

"Too slow for Billy," I agreed. "But faster than last week, and faster than Henry or Carlos." The other two boys I named were eleven. They were also in the Police Athletic League. Chico could give either of them more than they could handle in the ring.

Outside of the ring, the three boys were from different parts of the neighborhood. Geographically they should have been enemies, even at their young age. Because of the PAL, they beat each other up in the ring with padded gloves instead of flick knives on the streets.

The kids loved the gym. It was more home to

them than the houses they lived in. They knew Pops wouldn't let them in if he heard they had been fighting outside—and Pops always knew.

Pops made every kid who came through the door part of the Hawks tribe. He mixed them in with his own nine kids, just like they were family. They walked taller being Hawks, and they knew to be a Hawk, they had to behave a certain way.

To them, Pops was a lot like Father Tim had been to me and Mickey, only without the white collar. Instead of a gang of ruler-wielding nuns, Pops had me to back him up.

Pops had seen me fighting one night in a local smoker. When he found out I was also a cop, he recruited me to help him run the Central Division PAL.

The police department sponsored PALs at each division, taking in the neighborhood kids, keeping them busy and safe. We fought the other division PALs in tournaments. It was a rare fight when one of the Hawks lost on points.

Billy Two-Shoes was one of three American Indian kids from the Chumash tribe in the Central Division PAL. He was also something special. The PAL was sponsoring Billy in the Golden Gloves, but Pops himself made sure Billy's family had food and a roof so Billy could fight instead of work to support them.

Pops made pennies go a long way. During his time as a cop, he'd found out where a lot of skeletons were hidden. He rattled them gently whenever there was a need. Nobody said no to Pops.

I unbuckled Chico's headgear and pulled his gloves off. His hands were so small I did it without unlacing them. I tossed him a towel. He put it around his neck, holding onto the ends like he'd seen older boys do.

"Pops put you in against Billy because he knows you can take it," I said. "He knows it will make you better."

Chico nodded, not sure if he believed what I was saying.

"Who else your age has sparred with Billy?"

Chico shrugged.

"Nobody, that's who," I said. "Pops thinks you got it. So do I."

Chico looked at me, wanting it to be true. "Verdad?" he asked, his voice low.

"Yeah, verdad," I said. Truth. I held the ropes apart and he climbed out. I threw a punch at him. Chico blocked it and shuffled left ready to let loose a jab.

"Perfect," I said. "Now, clean up the spit buckets and then shower." He sauntered off with a smile, a little taller, a little more confident.

"Flynn," Pops called loudly, his voice filled with his normal raspy aggravation. "Come here."

I ducked between the ring ropes and joined Pops and Billy. Over their shoulders, I saw Bonnie Wallace come into the gym. She drew some stares as the gym wasn't usually habituated by women, but Bonnie ignored them and nodded in my direction. I held up a finger, acknowledging I'd seen her.

Pops was talking at me. "Set up southpaw and let Billy run some combinations."

I was wearing chinos, a sweatshirt, and high-top Converse sneakers. "My hands aren't wrapped," I said, looking at the gloves Pops was holding out.

"I'm not asking you to hit him; I'm asking him to hit you."

Nobody says no to Pops. I shoved my hands into the gloves.

Southpaw wasn't a problem for me. I was just as comfortable fighting left-handed as I was fighting out of an orthodox stance. It was just the way my brain worked. I sometimes switched in the middle of a round, which reigned confusion on my opponents.

Billy hadn't fought anybody who was a southpaw. He was a tall, rangy, kid with pitch black straight hair falling into his eyes. He was a confident fighter, and fast, but I knew my set up was throwing him off.

"You have to reverse your brain," I told him. Keeping my right in his face, I turned him the opposite way to his normal attack. "Think of it like fighting your mirror image."

"Flynn..." I heard a new voice call my name and turned to see who it was. Billy stepped around my right lead and threw a jab into my nose. Blood exploded.

Without hesitating, I threw a roundhouse left, striking Billy over his right ear. I twisted my punch at the last moment, so I hit him with the inside of my fist. Even though he was wearing headgear, the force of the blow shorted out his brain and turned his legs to rubber.

Slack-faced, Billy staggered backward like a puppet with half its strings cut. Pops moved in quickly to support him, but he was grinning. He knew Billy's cheap shot had earned him a painful lesson.

As far as Billy was concerned, the blow came out of nowhere. Getting hit in the nose stopped most people in their tracks. The pain was intense, plus there was the shock of the blood – your blood.

That was the reaction Billy's cockiness made him expect. However, I'd lost track of the times my nose had been mashed. It hurt, but it was far from disabling. Over the years, I'd also bled a body's worth of my own blood. It didn't faze me anymore.

Billy was a good fighter, excellent for his age. However, there was a lot of difference between dominating peers in PAL's tournaments and sparring with somebody who'd fought in streets, bars, and rings for fifteen years. My punch was harder and faster than anything Billy had ever faced before in his fights. Plus, he was a bantamweight, between 118 pounds and 126 pounds. I weighed in near the top of the scale for a middleweight, between 160 and 175 pounds.

When he regained his senses, he'd even realize I'd pulled the punch at the last second. If he were as good as Pops hoped, he wouldn't forget the lesson.

I didn't forget it when Father Tim taught it to me the same way.

Holding a towel beneath my nose and pinching the bridge, I made my way over to the ropes. A uniformed police sergeant I didn't recognize was looking up at me from ringside. The shiny name tag over his right uniform shirt pocket read, Mc-Culley.

"Sorry," he said, realizing he'd distracted me.

"No need," I said. "The kid had to learn the lesson sometime. Also, I should know better than to look away when I'm in the ring."

McCulley smiled, looking at the blood on my sweatshirt. "The chief wants to see you," he said.

"Chief Parker?"

"You work for another one?"

"No," I said, climbing out of the ring. "Give me a minute."

"Don't take long," McCulley said. "He wants to see you now."

I walked over to where Bonnie was standing. She held out an ice bag from Pops' small freezer. I took the bloody towel from my nose and replaced it with the ice bag. I tossed the towel on top of a stack Pops' daughter Tina was carrying to the laundry. She'd been in my corner during the Carter bout. She stuck her tongue out at me.

She was a rascal, but it came from being an only girl with eight brothers. I think Pops must have loved her more, but he didn't treat her any different than his sons. She'd even spent some time with the gloves on, holding her own against any of the PAL's kids her age.

I looked back at Bonnie. She was tall and poverty thin despite being comfortably well off from the earnings of other women. She was also smart, knew how to do business, and kept her girls as safe as she could.

She had more dirt on city politicians than Pops did, but she kept a low profile, ran her house clean, and didn't make waves. It was her formula for success in a world where Negro women were hardly allowed to exist.

I always worried, however, she would have to eventually pay the piper in some fashion. It was the nature of her profession.

We'd met when I rolled on a call where two of her girls had found themselves in a bind with a customer who was demanding more than they were willing to give. When I got there, the customer, a big 'ol boy who thought he was a fighter, decided he could mop the floor with me. I proved different, and he woke up in jail on an assault charge.

I figured life was already difficult enough for the two girls and made sure they got home to Bonnie without problems. Bonnie and I had been friends ever since.

"Rodney get on the bus?" I asked.

"I put him on myself," she said. "When I called Father Tim, he said to tell you he's heard from Mickey, a guy who practically has to get somebody else to write his letters for him, but he hasn't heard from you."

"I send money." I felt stung. I'd taken to school and absorbed reading and writing easily. Mickey had always struggled. Said he didn't care, but I knew he didn't understand why learning was so easy for me and not for him.

"Father Tim said you'd say that and to tell you money alone isn't enough."

"So, you came here to deliver a scolding from a priest."

"No, but it was fun," Bonnie said, then asked, "Did you know Rodney was a dip—a thief?"

"I know what a dip is," I said. "What did he pick-pocket from you?"

"Not from me. From one of the men who were beating him." Bonnie stepped closer and casually handed me an envelope. She was close enough for me to smell her faint perfume.

"He say which one he took it from?"

"He said the tall one he kicked."

Cooper. A good thief always takes advantage of a distraction, and I'd been distracted dealing with Tellis.

"He said it was in the inside jacket pocket."

I opened the envelope and looked inside. There were five twenty-dollar bills. I didn't understand.

I hefted the envelope. "You know what's in here?"

"I don't know how he knew, but Rodney said they were counterfeit."

I opened the envelope again and rubbed one of the bills between my fingers without taking it out.

"Maybe," I said. "But they're good enough to pass. This is a fortune to a kid like Rodney if he played it right."

"He said nobody would believe a kid like him would have a twenty-dollar bill without having stolen it. He also said nobody ever stood up for him before. He said he owed you."

I wondered if he'd still feel the same way once Father Tim got hold of him.

"Thanks," I said to Bonnie.

"You're not surprised I didn't keep 'em," she said, but her eyes were smiling.

"I know you better," I said.

"You just think you do." She turned to walk away. "And stop bringing me your strays. I run a business, not a charity."

The tone of her voice gave lie to the statement. If I brought them, she'd take them in.

"You done?" McCulley asked from behind me. He was a barrel-chested guy, who looked as if he was swaggering even when he was standing still.

I took the ice bag off my nose. The bleeding had stopped. I swallowed a gob of blood.

The chief.

My stomach churned. Not from the blood but thinking the arrests from the night before might have more fallout than I'd expected.

ROUND FOUR

Thirty minutes later, McCulley dropped me in front of the Bradbury Building at Third and Broadway, where the chief had his office.

The new Police Administration building, at First Street and Los Angeles Avenue, had been under construction for almost ten years. There had been uncountable delays for everything from funding to labor strikes, but the imposing seven-story structure was finally set to open sometime in the next year. Until then, the various police administration units remained scattered throughout different downtown buildings.

Inside the Bradbury, I'd waited for the exposed elevator to wind down to the ground floor. The operator opened the collapsible gate and let me in.

Creaking and groaning, the elevator reluctantly wound up to the fourth floor. It took forever. I didn't know what to expect, but I felt I might be better off if the elevator cable snapped.

The chief's office had a reception room where I was told by his secretary to take a seat. Fifteen minutes later, I was still wiggling around on one of the hard chairs. It was clear from the secretary's face that I should have put more effort into my appearance. I'd had a white dress shirt and tie at the gym along with a worn sports coat. I'd put them on with my chinos, which I now saw had a spray of tiny blood spots on one leg.

Eventually, the pebbled glass of the chief's inner sanctum opened slowly. Nobody came out, but the secretary gave me a permissive nod. I stood, took a deep breath, and went to answer the bell.

The only contact I'd ever had with Chief Parker was when I'd been standing at attention during graduation from the police academy. Parker had walked past me and forty other rookies as part of a ceremonial inspection. He had hard, cold, eyes, which were deep set in a fleshy face. The small round lenses of his glasses drew even more attention to the intensity of his stare.

Now, as I stood in front of his desk, he examined me with the same look. I heard somebody move behind me. He must have been hidden by the door when I stepped in. My scalp prickled.

The office was basic, nothing more than a working space. The chief was sitting behind a large oak desk, which sported scarred legs and an explosion of papers across the top.

The chief didn't get up.

I could feel a presence looming behind me. I forced myself not to turn around. I did not like the way this was going. I liked being a cop. I thought I was a good cop. I didn't want to have it taken away.

The chief eyed me speculatively. "Do you own a suit, Officer Flynn?"

I gulped. "Yes, sir, but this was all I had with me when Sergeant McCulley came to get me…" I knew I was blathering.

"Enough," Parker said, waving his hand dismissively before moving on. "I think you know Detective Jones." The chief came down hard on the word detective and nodded his head toward the person behind me.

I turned, not surprised to see the tall Negro with the tuft of white in his hair.

"Cornel Jones," he said in a deep voice. "Call me Tombstone." He didn't offer his hand, but he gave me a huge grin, showing where his moniker came from. His teeth were horse sized. The front two flat slabs of ivory were half-mooned at the top by pink gums. They looked exactly like cemetery grave markers.

Up close, you could see he was built to fit his

teeth. He was at least six-foot-five. Where he was standing, I couldn't see the door behind him.

I turned back to the chief.

He was standing up.

"Give me your badge, Officer Flynn," Chief Parker said, delivering the KO blow with a demanding hand held out flat.

I felt like Billy had when I'd delivered the roundhouse left. My legs were shaky, and I struggled not to fall down and kiss the canvas.

I swallowed hard. The fingers on the chief's outstretched palm waggled a give it to me statement without words. "That was an order, Officer Flynn."

I reached into my back pocket and pulled out the leather wallet where I carried my badge when off duty. I placed it in the chief's palm.

He flipped the wallet open and looked at the metal oval with the word Policeman curved above a relief of LA City Hall. In the center of the relief was an enameled circle containing the city seal. The words Los Angeles Police curved in the opposite direction below the seal. Finally, just above the bottom, was the badge number—138.

It was just a hunk of metal, but I felt like I'd taken a hundred body blows when I gave it up.

Chief Parker tapped the badge absently. "When you came on the job four years ago, I'm sure you heard the rumors I was in bed with Bugsy Siegel."

I had, but I thought it was best to keep my mouth shut. Parker was all about cleaning up the LAPD, so I wasn't sure how true they were. I'd never seen any indication he was in bed with organized crime, but then I didn't run in the higher circles of administration.

The chief pulled open the middle drawer of his desk and dropped my badge into it. "Siegel was the mob's west coast capo. He was as vicious and crazy as everyone said. He brought Mickey Cohen up as his lieutenant. Sort of like Hitler trying to get Satan on his side."

Tombstone chimed in from behind me. "They say when you sup with the devil you better use a long spoon."

"Too true," the chief agreed.

"There was one good thing about Siegel," the chief continued. "He needed to keep organized gambling out of LA. If he didn't, then his little oasis in the Nevada desert would shrivel and die. So, Siegel and I had a deal. I let him live in LA, and he did a Big Greenie and squealed whenever the east coast would send a heavy out west to start numbers running or illegal gaming in my city."

I knew Big Greenie was Harry Greenberg. He been a mob informant and got himself taken out in a hail of bullets. Siegel supposedly orchestrated the hit on orders from Louis Lepke Buchalter, boss of Murder, Inc. Siegel had been arrested for ordering the hit, but Whitey Krakower, the trigger man, was killed before getting to trial. No surprise there. The conspiracy charges against Siegel were dropped.

"Siegel had to know what was coming," Parker went on. "But he was obsessed with getting Las Vegas off the ground. He'd tell me when the mob was sending somebody west, and my Hat Squad boys would meet them at the train station or airport. They'd take 'em up and show 'em Mulholland Falls, and send 'em home with their tails between their legs."

Mulholland Drive cuts across the tops of the hills separating LA from the farms and suburbs of the San Fernando Valley. There were no waterfalls there. Showing somebody Mulholland Falls meant taking them up to the top of Mulholland Drive and tossing them off.

They would crash through the scrub and bushes covering the hills until they landed on the road where it switched back on itself. Whoever took the trip down the falls would then be taken, bandaged and broken, back to the train station or airport and sent back home. Once someone had experienced Mulholland Falls, they never seemed eager to make a return visit.

Tombstone had come around to stand on one side of the chief's desk. "Chief, I think Officer Flynn here is wondering why you're telling him all this."

The chief looked over at him. "You can find yourself back in uniform patrolling Harbor Division as easy as snapping my fingers."

"Come on, Chief," Tombstone gave up his big smile again. "You need me to show you be progressive."

"You aren't the only Negro on this department."

"But I'm the biggest...and the best dressed..."

I figured Parker would explode, but he just laughed. "You are, you are," he said. He turned back to me. "I'll get to the point. Siegel is old news. Siegel could be controlled because he needed something. Cohen is a different story. You know what Cohen did the night after Siegel was hit?"

Everybody knew. It was legend. "He shot up the lobby of the Ambassador Hotel," I said. "He demanded Siegel's murderer come out and play, but there were no takers."

"A pretty gutsy move, huh?" Parker asked.

"I guess..."

"It is—unless you were the one who hit Siegel yourself."

That shut me up. Nobody was ever arrested for Siegel's murder. It happened in Beverly Hills, outside of LAPD's jurisdiction.

The chief nodded knowingly. "Cohen isn't Siegel. He's far worse, a mad dog who wants to make this city wide open for every vice there is. And I'm going to stop him. Not all at once, but one step at a time until Cohen is either inside or under the sod."

He reached into the desk drawer where he had thrown my badge and took something out. He tossed it to me.

I juggled it but stopped it from falling to the floor. It was metal and oval. I turned it over. It was a Detective badge.

In physical form, it wasn't much different from my policeman badge. It simply had the word Detective etched where Policeman had been on my other badge. However, the effective difference between the two badges couldn't be calculated.

"I'm promoting you, Flynn," the chief said.

"I passed the test?" I felt shell-shocked.

"Not if you mean that waste of time written test you took. You passed my personal detective test Friday night when you didn't take a dive against Cohen's prospect, Carter."

I looked over at Tombstone. "Cohen didn't send that note?"

Tombstone just smiled. "Had to see what you were made of."

I looked back at the chief.

"Did you know you were up against Cohen's men last night?" Parker asked.

"Sure. I recognized two of them."

"They try to get you to back down?"

I shrugged.

"Why didn't you arrest the kid they were beating on?" Parker asked.

"What was the point?" I asked back.

Tombstone chuckled. "He bedded him down at Bonnie Wallace's place. Paid to put him on a bus to the same orphanage in Chicago where he grew up."

I felt embarrassed. "I'm going to have to talk to Bonnie about telling tall tales."

"If she hadn't, you might not be here," Parker said, bringing my attention back to him.

"Is this for real?" I asked, hefting the detective badge.

"As long as you do exactly what I tell you to do."

"What might that be?"

The chief chuckled. "First, you're going to be partners with the only negro detective on the LAPD. Is that a problem?"

I looked at Tombstone. "No, sir," I said.

"Then let me give you a problem. A big one. I need you to go into the ring and knock out Solomon King."

ROUND FIVE

It took a moment of shock before the chief's statement sunk in. When it did, it still didn't make sense. And if it had, I might have handed him back the detective badge. I wasn't sure I wanted it that bad.

"Do you know what a policeman is in boxing slang?" Parker asked me.

"A fighter who other fighters have to get through in order to get a shot at the champ," I said.

"Well, you're going to be Archie Moore's policeman," Parker said, referring to the current light-heavyweight champ.

"Willy Stevenson already has the job," I said. Stevenson was a fighter past his prime. He'd never challenge Moore for the championship, but he was a tenacious and smart fighter. Anybody wanting a shot at Moore had to beat Stevenson first.

"Okay, then you're going to be the fighter Solomon King has to go through to get to Stevenson. And you're not going to let him."

"Why not let Stevenson handle King?"

Tombstone weighed in. "Stevenson can't handle King."

"And you think I can?" I was feeling exasperated. "I'm not even a pro. I'm an amateur middleweight. Nobody is going to let me in the ring against King. It's ridiculous."

Parker gave me his hard stare. "I've heard about your boxing record in the navy, both official and unofficial. They say you never backed down or went down, not even when you were up against much bigger men." He shrugged. "But if you don't want the job..." He held out his hand.

The detective badge felt hot and heavy in my fist.

Tombstone spoke again. "You at the top weight for your class. Ten pounds of muscle will see you up to light-heavyweight."

Chief Parker picked up the pitch. "I've got people with the Boxing Commission," he said. "Your license to fight pro comes along with the badge."

"I still don't see how this gets me on a card against King," I said.

"One step at a time. You've got six weeks before you fight Trevor Haywood at the Olympic. It's a done deal. Once you put Haywood down, you'll fight King."

I shook my head. "No way King's camp is going

to be interested in fighting some guy with one pro win," I said. "Assuming I even get past Haywood. And I'm not fighting somebody who's going to take a dive if that's what you're planning."

"Haywood is on his way to Palookaville," Tombstone said. "He'll fight square, but you'll get past him."

"Neither Stevenson's nor Moore's managers want their fighters to go up against King," Chief Parker said. "Both camps have agreed not to accept a fight with King until he faces you."

"Okay, this is still crazy. I don't understand the point," I said.

"What point?" the chief asked.

"Why I'm fighting King in the first place?"

"Boxing is crooked enough without letting Cohen get his claws in," Parker said. "Cohen is a cancer on this city. I'm going to see him taken down. Every time he flexes his muscle to expand his crime empire, I'm going to be there to thwart him."

"You shut down King," Tombstone said, "and there's no way Cohen will get a championship fight for him. Then, we put pressure on Cohen's machine everywhere else, and he be too busy to find another prospect."

"How about you get in the ring with King," I said to Tombstone. I was feeling testy.

"My momma didn't raise m to be a fool," he said, showing his teeth in that grin I was already beginning to find irritating.

"So, that's it?" I asked the chief. "I'm a fool?"

"You're my fool," Chief Parker said. "A blue fool. You in or out?"

I heaved a sigh. This wasn't how I saw myself making detective. Then I felt something inside me click. I felt suddenly strong. It had been too long since I'd actually fought for something. Nobody could possibly believe I could beat King, but it seemed both Tombstone and Chief Parker felt otherwise. What did I believe?

I looked over at Tombstone, raising my chin at him. "Where do I get one of those fancy hats?"

ROUND SIX

Pops was delighted when he found out the details of Chief Parker's crazy plan.

"I finally got me a contender," he said before rushing off to find his wife, Mama Hawk, to get her started feeding me correctly.

I had to put on ten pounds to qualify as a light-heavyweight, but it had to be ten pounds of muscle and quick, not fat and slow.

"Isn't Mickey Cohen going to know this is a set-up?" I asked Tombstone. It was something that had been bothering me since the beginning. "It's going to be kind of hard to hide the fact I'm a cop."

"Don't make no never-mind," Tombstone said. "He know you a cop, but he also gonna know if he wants to get his boy a championship fight, he gonna have to go through you."

I shook my head, still caught off guard by it all. Yesterday, I had been fighting just because being a fighter was what I was. Today, I suddenly had a cause, a reason. It was a reason beyond survival, like when I was a kid, and a reason beyond simply getting to the next fight. I had a reason to win, and I was going against the odds, way against the odds. I felt right at home.

Tombstone had been correct, Trevor Haywood was a fighter on his way down. He was a good fighter, but not a great fighter. The fact his camp would accept a fight with me under these circumstances spoke loud and clear. They were desperate for easy targets to get him back on track.

I couldn't take Haywood lightly. He'd fought over twenty light-heavyweight bouts with a record of 10-8-2. Six of his ten wins had been by KO, but the two losses in his last two fights told the story. He had a stunning right cross. I'd have to be very careful not to get in front of it. But if I could put on the weight and maintain my quickness, I should be able to dance around him.

From the gym, Tombstone took me along to Del Floria's Clothing, a menswear store in the middle of the downtown garment district. Del Floria's was a wholesaler, but they were known to be good to police—meaning they sold directly to cops at wholesale or below.

Getting out of the car, I asked Tombstone about the tuft of white hair, which fell like a comma over his forehead.

"Knife wound," he said. His voice was clipped, telling me I'd asked a too personal question. He was telling me we weren't friends yet. "Hair grew back white."

The tone of his response told me not to ask how he received the knife wound, so I silently accepted what he said and followed him into the menswear store.

Del Floria was a fussy little first-generation Italian. He'd taken over the business from his father, who had immigrated from Sicily. It was in his blood, he said. His grandfather had been in the rag trade back in the old country. He told me all of this within the first minute of entering the store with Tombstone.

Del Floria might have been willing to give cops a good discount, but Tombstone clearly made him nervous. Since I didn't have any clothes of my own to go along with my new detective status, the little Italian whisked me into a couple of off-the-rack suits. Then he rounded things out with shirts, shoes, ties, and socks. Even with the police discount, the total made a large dent in my bank account—especially when I added in the cost of a black felt, wide-brimmed, Borsalino fedora. I was starting to feel my oats.

Chief Parker had explained that Tombstone and I were on probation with The Gangster Squad. We wouldn't be working with the others until we successfully shut down Mickey Cohen's plans for the fight game. If we completed the job successfully, we were in. If we didn't, we'd still be detectives, but we wouldn't be playing with the big boys. I bought the Borsalino on faith.

Outside of Del Floria's, I loaded my purchases into the back of the dark green detective sedan Tombstone had been leaning against the night before. I then settled myself on the front passenger seat.

Tombstone didn't start the engine immediately. I looked over at him.

"It really don't bother you I'm driving, does it?" he asked.

I was confused. "Why should it?"

Tombstone shook his head and turned the key. The engine rumbled into life. "My cousin told me you were this way. Said you didn't see coloreds like most white folks."

"Who's your cousin?"

"Calvin Arlo Washington."

I shook my head. "Never heard of him."

"He's a big boy," Tombstone said. "Bigger than me. He got himself into a little scrap with some

Southern crackers while on shore leave in a little know-nothing bar along the Yangtze River."

Suddenly, I remembered. "A Navy gob," I said. "Didn't quite understand how odds worked. One on twenty rarely comes out in your favor."

"That's my cousin. All he wanted was a drink, but the crackers didn't like the way the Chinese barmaid was paying attention to him."

"Didn't help they were from a different ship."

Tombstone was cruising through the light traffic. "Calvin said you walked through the door like you was ten feet tall. Started throwing sailors off him like they was kids on a playground."

"They were drunk and mean. I was sober and meaner. Attitude and a stout truncheon were all I needed."

Tombstone nodded. "Calvin said you didn't stop with the crackers."

I smiled at the memory. "Nope. Calvin was drunk and mean, too. He squared off on me."

"And you took him down..."

"Like chopping down a redwood."

"He also told me he woke up the next morning in his rack instead of the brig. Heard later the crackers weren't so lucky."

"His ship was leaving. Also, he didn't start the fight."

"But he was Negro."

I looked at Tombstone. "Is that what this is about?" I'd figured this was coming. Somehow it always did in one form or another. "I don't care what color you are. You do your job, you cover my back, and I'll do the same for you. I got enough problems right now fighting Haywood, let alone Solomon King. If you have a problem with my lily-white skin, then grow up and get over it."

Tombstone laughed. It was a full-throated sound, rich and deep. "You is too much. I hope your fists be as fast as your mouth."

"I'm serious," I said. "Are you in my corner on this or not? Are you going to be my partner or not?"

Every cop knew there was a difference between partners and just some cop with whom you were assigned to work. Partners went deeper, as deep as the bone and beyond.

Sometimes, cop partnerships built over time and shared experiences. Sometimes, they happened instantaneously—a manly version of love at first sight. A partner was somebody you would lay your life down for without even thinking about it because you knew, without question, he would do the same for you. Partners were bonded. It was deeper than marriage. You either had it with the guy you worked with or you didn't.

I wasn't stupid. I knew somebody like Tombstone faced racism every day. But I'd faced it too. Every day of growing up there was somebody who hated Mickey and me because our last name was Irish. The Polish kids hated us. The Jewish kids hated us. Even other Irish kids hated us. And I hated them.

Father Tim beat the hate out of me and out of Mickey. He didn't beat it out of us with a stick or a belt. He beat it out of us in the ring. He taught us being a man had nothing to do with the color of your skin or in what country your family originated.

Being a man had to do with standing up when you got knocked down, with always doing what you said you were going to do, and with fighting fair. Never cheat, never take what wasn't yours, and never, never, back down from a challenge.

Tombstone pulled the car over to the curb and put the steering column mounted gear shift into park. He turned this whole torso in his seat to look at me. His face was a carved ebony mask.

"I've never trusted a white man in my life."

"Seems you trust the chief," I said.

"Only so far," Tombstone said. "He is stirring the pot by promoting me, but at least he's honest about it."

"So, what's it going to take?"

There was a beat of silence, and then Tombstone stuck out his hand. I looked at it for a second. It was a huge mitt. I put my own hand into it. Tombstone's grip was firm, not crushing; he wasn't out to prove anything.

"Partners," he said. It wasn't a question.

"Partners," I said.

ROUND SEVEN

After four weeks of hard training, I was getting into a rhythm—up at six and out the door for six miles of roadwork. Then a full breakfast at Mama Hawk's table. She found ways to load calories into fruits, cheeses, eggs, and rare meat like nobody's business.

While breakfast settled, I talked strategy with Pops, who'd dug up some raw films of Trevor Haywood in action. Some fight venues had recently started filming bouts. Somehow, Pops had managed to get himself access.

In the late morning, I'd start in on one of Pops' specially designed workouts. Everything was about keeping me fast. He had me on the speed back and the dodge bag, but he was also working my abdominals. No weightlifting, but loads of isometric exercises. After lunch, I'd work up a sweat again on the heavy bag and then get into the ring to spar with Donovan Hawks, Pops' eldest son, who was a heavyweight Golden Gloves contender and

Olympic team hopeful.

At twenty-one, Donovan was strong and cocky, a lot like Billy Two-Shoes only more experienced. When I was sparring with Donovan, I always got the feeling he felt he was the better man—believing it should be him going in the ring against Haywood for a shot at Solomon King.

The fight with Haywood was only two weeks away, and I was still five pounds underweight. Mama Hawks cooking wasn't to blame. I was working so hard I was burning all the fuel she put into me. Pops wasn't about to let me ease off until a few days before the bout, but he assured me he had a plan to help me make weight.

Chief Parker had been as good as his word. The Boxing Commission had come through with my license, and Willie Stevenson's and Archie Moore's camps were stonewalling Cohen when it came to scheduling a match with Solomon King. Cohen was supposedly fit to be tied, but there was nothing he could do.

The chief made it clear he didn't want me or Tombstone doing other police work on the street unless it was connected in some way to the fight with Solomon King. This made my training a priority, and Tombstone was always there with Pops to help out.

That morning, Pops had me on the heavy bag early. I was working intervals—forty seconds of punching, twenty seconds of rest, and back to punching again. With his jacket off, tie lowered, and sleeves rolled up, Tombstone was leaning in to steady the bag. He was always around, watching, helping, supporting. If he resented taking a backseat to my fighting, he didn't show it.

"Make it pop!" Pops said.

"I am making it pop," I said, hitting the bag with a hard left.

Pops pushed me out of the way. "I said make it pop, not flop."

Pops shot out a right jab from the middle of his squat body and the bag popped! Tombstone was forced to take a step backward to keep control of the heavy bag.

"How long is it gonna be before you learn? You're still hitting from your shoulders," Pops said, turning to me with frustration on his face. "That's good enough for drunks and pugs, but you're getting into the ring with a heavyweight contender."

Pops maneuvered me back in front of the bag. He put his hand on my right hip and another on my right shoulder, as he'd done a hundred times before.

"Slowly throw your right," he said.

I threw the punch.

"Slowly!" Pops yelled.

I threw the right in slow motion. As I did so, Pops pushed my shoulder and twisted my hip into the punch.

I almost fell over my own feet. Tombstone wasn't helping things. He didn't laugh, but he did give up one of those wide, full-toothed, irritating grins of his.

"You see what I want you to do?" Pops asked.

"Yeah, punch from my shoulder and my hips..."

"No! No! No!" Pops raised his fists and his eyes Heavenward. "What happened when you twisted your shoulder and your hips into the punch?"

I must have looked blank because Pops started kicking at me. "Your feet...your feet!"

I was bouncing away from him when Pops stopped chasing me and turned to Tombstone. "You tell him," he said.

"I think he wants you to punch from your feet." Tombstone upped the wattage of his grin.

"I want you to punch all the way from the canvas!" Pops yelled at me.

I nodded like I knew what he was talking about.

"You've got a punch like a mule kick in your own weight class," Pops said in a calmer tone. "But a heavyweight is going to think you're a gnat bothering him. These guys are mountains of mean and stupid. You've got to hit them with everything you've got, plus the canvas underneath your feet."

Pops threw a slow motion right, overemphasizing everything he did.

"Think about your fist like a bullet in your gun. It's harmless unless there's power behind it, a primer to set the powder off, a firing pin to strike the primer, a hammer behind the pin, a trigger to drop the hammer, fingers to pull the trigger, a hand to steady the fingers, and an arm to guide the hand." When Pops' punch was fully extended, his whole body had been behind moving it to its final position.

Pops threw the same slow punch again. "Your fist is backed by your wrist, which is backed by your arm, which comes from the shoulder, which twists in from the power in your hips, which delivers the power from your buttocks, which is driven by your thigh, which is turned by your knee, your calf, your ankle, and your foot, which draws power from the canvas beneath it..."

As Pops finished talking, his fist was three inches from the leather of the hanging heavy bag. Suddenly, his whole body snapped, twisting from his feet, his fist exploding across the remaining distance to the leather.

The bag popped, jinking up in the air on its chain.

Kinetic energy flowed through the bag, knocking a grunt out of the unprepared Tombstone and staggering him backward.

"You learn to hit like that," Pops said to me. "And ain't nobody big enough to stay on their feet."

He turned to walk away. "Keep at it," he said over his shoulder. "Five more sets of intervals. And this time punch from the canvas!"

An hour later, Pops called for the end of the morning training. There'd be sparring again with Donovan in the late afternoon, but until then Tombstone and I had some Cohen connected police work to do.

After Tombstone and I had our little heart to heart several weeks earlier, we'd gone to the small apartment I was renting, moving most of my things over to a spare room above Ten Hawks Gym. Pops owned the building and lived above it with Mama Hawk, Tina, and whichever of the interchangeable male Hawk siblings were still at home. But there was still space for me, even though I would be using the gym's locker room downstairs to shower.

Everyone agreed it was going to be a better arrangement for training and for Mama Hawk to keep feeding me up. Apparently, Chief Parker had a slush fund available for food and training fees and whatever else we were going to need in our campaign.

Even after showering, my arms were sore from the intervals on the heavy bag. I could hardly bring them up in front of me. Dressed in one of my new suits, I met Tombstone outside the gym. He was leaning against the fender of our detective sedan drinking a soda out of a bottle.

"That old man can really hit," he said. "I swear, my chest feels bruised from that last pop of his."

"So, my feeble efforts had nothing to do with how you feel?"

Tombstone shook his head. "You've got a ways to go before you hitting with that kind of dynamite. But you better get to it quick."

I reached into the inside pocket of my suit, removing the envelope Bonnie Wallace had given to me. I'd been too busy training to think about what to do with the counterfeit bills, but I'd decided to finally get to it.

I handed the envelope to Tombstone.

"What's this?" he asked, taking it. His face clouded over when he looked inside. "We don't take no payoffs," he said. His voice was hard. There was a disappointed, almost hurt tone to it.

"Never have. Never will," I said.

Tombstone stared steadily at me, the envelope still in his hand.

"Take a closer look," I said.

He dropped his eyes to the contents of the envelope. With his other hand, he riffled through the
bills. He took one of the twenties out and held it up
toward the sun, trying to look through it.

"Counterfeit?"

"If you have to ask, then they're very good counterfeits."

He grunted and put the bill back in the envelope
with the others.

"Okay, so what do these have to do with anything?" he asked.

I told him where they came from.

"The kid just gave 'em up?"

"Figured he'd either get them stolen from him or
get him beat for being black and having them."

Tombstone nodded. He handed the envelope
back to me. I slid it back into my jacket pocket.

"You've been holding on to those for a while?"

"Too much other stuff going on," I said. "But I
think it's time to see if we can use them."

"How so?" he asked.

"Taking out Mickey Cohen's light-heavyweight
prospect might upset the big man, but it really isn't
going to hurt him. It might stop him from spreading
his influence to the fight game, but his organized
crime machine will still keep on turning in L.A."

"The bills were taken off one of Cohen's thugs,"

Tombstone said, picking up my train of thought.

"If we can find the source of the counterfeits," I said, "maybe we can put the hurt on Cohen's machine. Really cost him."

"Get us a few steps closer to closing him down altogether."

"Maybe cost him enough to put him in bad with the bent nose boys back east."

Tombstone grinned. "Maybe they do our job for us."

"Maybe," I said. "Cohen is a weasel. He'd probably find some way out of the corner, but we'll make him sweat."

"You're really going to be raising your profile with him."

"You too," I said. "Can you stand the heat?"

"I'm black. I've been taking heat all my life."

"You're not married," I said. "Anybody else close?"

"I've got a sister, but she's back in Alabama," Tombstone said. "No way Cohen could find her there. I know you ain't got a wife, and I ain't seen you sneaking off to meet a girlfriend these past few weeks..."

"Too tired," I said, and we both laughed.

"Footloose, that's me," I said.

"We'll see how footloose you are if Cohen comes

gunning for us. He be a rabid dog," Tombstone said.

"So, we have to be prepared," I said.

Tombstone gave me his silent assessing stare. It was as if he could see into my head, checking he could trust what I said.

"Where do you want to start with this counterfeiting thing?" he asked.

"Treasury Department is supposed to investigate counterfeiting. Their office is in the Federal Building on the Westside. Why don't we pay them a visit?"

ROUND EIGHT

We were looking dapper in our fedoras and slick suits, but those items didn't make us stand out in the crowd moving through the lobby of the Federal Building. Both Tombstone and I were fighting the uncomfortable feeling of being country cousins visiting upscale relatives. City boys up against the feds.

Feeling uncomfortable was agitating. This was our city. The Feds didn't even have local powers of arrest in Los Angeles, or anywhere else in the state of California. If the feds wanted to make a pinch or serve a warrant, they had to come to us, hat in hand, and ask if we'd go with them to make things legal. They were the feds, and they didn't like that one little bit. Between federal agencies and city agencies, there was always bad juju.

Tombstone and I didn't think we were going to get much cooperation, but we could stir the pot and see what we could learn.

The elevator opened, and there she was...The redhead from ringside who had been sitting next to Mickey Cohen, studying me. The one I thought I'd recognized.

She had her head up, and I saw her eyes widen when she saw me. Even dressed up with my Borsalino at a rakish angle, she knew me. No doubt. And I knew her, but I still couldn't place her.

She dropped her head, breaking eye contact. She turned her body sideways, slipping between Tombstone and me like a rabbit dashing down a hole. I turned toward her, but her heels were clacking across the lobby tiles and she was out the door. There was nothing left of her, but a trace of magnolia scent and the memory of nicely nyloned legs and a woman's sway.

"You coming?" Tombstone asked from inside the elevator.

I joined him with my mind spinning all the way to the third floor. I knew the redhead but from where? If she was hanging out with Cohen, it could be important. And, if she was hanging out with Cohen, what was she doing at the Federal Building?

I had to push thoughts of her face and body out of my mind as I followed Tombstone out of the elevator and into the office of the Treasury Department. We flashed our badges at the pinched looking secretary and were quickly ushered into the office of the Special Agent in Charge.

"Walter Dent," said the SAC, introducing himself with an outstretched hand stretching across his government-issue desk. He was a bulky man in a gray suit. His cheeks were pockmarked and jowly, but his eyes were sharp and alert.

"What can the Treasury Department do for two of L.A.'s finest?" he asked once we did our part of the introductions and were sitting down.

I took the envelope out of my jacket pocket and removed one of the counterfeit twenty-dollar bills. I handed it to Dent. "Can you tell us anything about this bill?"

He glanced at the bill, rubbing it between the thumb and forefinger of his right hand. He then brought it up to his nose and sniffed it.

"I assume you know it's counterfeit?"

I nodded. Tombstone simply sat immobile. Even I found his stillness intimidating.

Dent glanced back at the bill. "It's a good counterfeit. The printing plates used were clean. The ink is an excellent match, but the paper is rough. Probably from a test batch. Counterfeiters don't waste good paper on samples; it's too hard to get."

"Not made to pass on the street?"

Dent shook his head. "Whoever printed this is

certainly planning on passing bills on the street. But this is only a sample to make sure the plates and ink are working. Do you have any others?"

I showed him the four bills remaining in the envelope. Dent stuck out his hand. I was reluctant, but I let him take the bills. He ran them through the same process as the first then stacked them with the other and placed them on his desk blotter.

"Can I ask where you got these?"

"You can ask," I said.

Dent's eyes narrowed. "Counterfeiting is a federal crime under the jurisdiction of the Treasury Department."

I tried Dent with a smile. "I didn't say I wouldn't tell you. I was just hoping for a little more give and take before I did. You haven't told us much yet we didn't already know."

Dent gave me a stare. "What's your interest?"

"You know us city boys," I said. "We blunder along rooting for truffles."

Tombstone suddenly leaned forward and snagged the pile of bills from the center of the desk. Dent moved a hand to stop him. If it had been a gunfight, Dent would have been dead and cooling on the ground.

"City property," Tombstone said.

"Now, look here," Dent started. He was leaning

forward definitely ruffled, one hand pointing a finger at us.

"Agent Dent," I said, cutting him off. "If you level with us, we'll cooperate." I looked over at Tombstone and tilted my head in the direction of Dent's desk. Tombstone reached out and replaced the bills on Dent's blotter.

Dent visibly relaxed. "Those bills are confirmation of something we've been waiting for. Six months ago, a man named Verne Chadwick was released from prison. He'd been sentenced for forging Treasury plates. He disappeared a month later. We believe he's back to his old trade. I'd have to have them examined further, but these bills look like his work."

"The bills came into our possession off a leg-breaker with ties to Mickey Cohen," I said.

"Makes sense," Dent said. "Cohen has the up-front money to get a counterfeiting operation off the ground on a large scale. Chadwick was once an engraver for the Treasury Department before he went bad. He is skilled and knows the process. He knows where to go for ink and paper."

I looked hard at Dent. "You already knew Cohen was behind this."

Dent shrugged. "Suspected. I told you, it makes sense. Although we haven't been able to locate

Chadwick, his trail led to L.A."

"What are you doing about it?" Tombstone asked.

Dent thought for a few seconds before replying. "We have an agent close to the source."

"Undercover?" I asked.

"Deep undercover," Dent said. "Any steps you take could put the agent in danger. This is a big operation. You need to let us run it."

Outside the Federal Building a few minutes later, Tombstone unlocked our sedan and opened the doors to let the heat out. The sun was high and shining. I felt a trickle of sweat run down my back. We'd got nothing more out of Dent, but we'd let him keep the bills anyway.

"We gonna let the feds run with this?" Tombstone asked.

The Treasury Department might have the counterfeiting experts, but this was still our city.

"We told Dent we would..."

"But..."

"But we might have lied to him since he lied to us."

"He did?"

"Yeah. He was careful to make us think his undercover agent is a man, but I think it's a woman. There's a problem, but I think I know who..."

Tombstone was quick on the uptake. "The dame

who turned your head when she got off the elevator?"

"Yes."

"Who is she?"

"That's the problem. I know her from somewhere, but I can't place her."

There was the sound of a saxophone, and I looked over at the plaza of the Federal Building where we had just been. A tall Negro in a shiny black suit and a porkpie hat was playing his sax softly, his back to the wall of the building. His sax case was open at his feet to catch change from passers-by. He'd have to move along quickly if a uniformed cop saw him, but he looked desperate enough to take the risk.

He could barely play the sax well enough for me to make out the tune, Someone To Watch Over Me...

And then I had it...

"Anita O'Shay!"

Tombstone gave me a funny look. "Who?"

"Anita O'Shay," I slapped the roof of the sedan, looking across it at Tombstone. "The woman... the one who came out of the elevator. Anita O'Shay. She's the new singer at the Blue Cat in Hollywood."

"Jazz club?"

"Yeah."

"You seen her?"

"No, but I saw posters a couple of months ago

outside the club advertising her coming appearance."

"You think a jazz singer is a female Treasury agent?"

"I don't know. But that's who she is. I saw her with Cohen, and again here at the Federal building. And I don't put much stock in coincidence."

ROUND NINE

I might have figured out who Anita O'Shay might be, but there wasn't any time before the fight with Trevor Haywood to find out if I was right. Pops kept my training regime rigid, and even Tombstone, as big as he was, didn't want to argue with him.

The Sunday before the Friday night fight, Pops gave me a rare day off. He still had me do a couple of miles of roadwork, some light calisthenics to stay loose, and exactly ten minutes in the steam room. I was still having problems putting on the needed weight, and Pops didn't want me sweating off any poundage.

With a little spare time, Tombstone and I took a trip out to the county jail where Ennis Cooper was being held. Cooper was the goon Rodney had taken the counterfeit bills from. He wasn't happy to see us.

He was still waiting to go before the judge on the outstanding assault warrant he'd been arrested on after our encounter. It could be another month before he got in a courtroom. The wheels of justice turned slow for repeat offenders like Cooper.

The guard brought him into the interview room, a concrete box with two chairs set in the middle. Over the chairs hung a harshly bright lightbulb in the center of a wide, flat, metal shade. Everything in the room was gray, including Cooper.

"What do you want?" he asked. His tone was belligerent as he sat in the chair facing the back wall. Tombstone leaned on the closed door behind him. I sat in the chair in front of Cooper.

"You don't look very good, Cooper," I said. "Prison life doesn't seem to agree with you."

Cooper looked like he'd lost ten pounds since the night I stopped him and his buddies from beating Rodney. His features were drawn to the point of gauntness.

"What would you know about it?"

I leaned forward, snapping out my right hand to grab Cooper's chin. "I know you've got the answer to a question."

"I ain't telling you nothing."

The words coming out of Cooper's mouth were slightly distorted by the hold I had on his chin.

I released him and sat back. "I want to know where you got the twenty dollar bills you had in your coat pocket."

A glint of fear flashed in Cooper's eyes. "I don't know what you're talking about."

I smiled, ignoring his statement. "You must have been wondering all this time what happened to the envelope with the bills. It wasn't booked into your property, and nobody has said a word about it since. Maybe you thought some copper got light-fingered and kept the money for himself. Maybe you thought you were home free."

"I told you, I don't know nothing about no counterfeit bills."

"I didn't say they were counterfeit."

Cooper looked cornered. He was starting to sweat. He turned in his chair, looking back at Tombstone. No help there.

I moved my chair closer to Cooper and leaned forward. I played a hunch. "You were a bad boy, weren't you, Cooper?"

"I didn't do nothing..."

"Do you know how many guys there are in prison who told me they didn't do nothing." My voice was lower, soothing. "I don't think you were supposed to have those bills. I think you snagged them when nobody was looking."

Sweat was beading heavily on Cooper's forehead. "I'm not saying anything. Do you know how long I'd last in here if it got out I squealed?"

I sat back in my chair again. I nodded as if I was thinking about it. "Do you know how long you'd last in here if I put the word out about you stealing those bills? Do you think Mickey Cohen would just let it pass?"

I saw Cooper's Adam's apple bob up and down as he swallowed. "Look, don't do that, okay?"

"Then tell me."

Cooper rubbed his hands over his face. "The bills were just sitting there, a mountain of them. We was supposed to burn 'em. Nobody was going to miss a handful. They was just samples."

"Where was this?"

"This guy, Chadwick, brought them in to show Mickey. He had 'em in a duffel bag. Told Mickey as soon as the good paper came in he was ready to roll."

"You're telling me this happened in Mickey's office?"

"Yeah. Mickey went crazy. Yelling at Chadwick for bringing the stuff. Told Tellis and me to take the stuff out and burn it and make sure there was nothing left."

"And you couldn't bear to see all that funny money going up in smoke?"

Cooper shrugged. "It looked good to me."

"Where does Mickey have Chadwick stashed?"

"I don't know..."

"Cooper," I let my voice take on an edge.

"I swear," Cooper implored me with open hands and spread arms. "I heard it was in the garment district downtown. Mickey runs a couple of sweat-shops down there. He uses the sound of the sewing machines to hide the sound of the printing press."

"You ever been there?"

"I'm telling you, no, never. I don't know."

I nodded. Nothing was ever easy.

ROUND TEN

Before I really knew it, the night of the Haywood fight was upon us. I was anxious, which was usual before a fight. Once the first blows were thrown and received nothing else would matter.

Boxing was one man versus another man, and Father Tim had taught both me and Mickey we were always man enough. Officially, I was stepping up tonight. Not only entering the pro ranks but moving into the world of the light-heavyweights. However, back at the orphanage and all the way through my Shore Patrol duties and beyond, I'd fought whoever had come my way. Bigger, badder, meaner, two guys, three guys, more, it didn't matter.

I'd needed to fight. Getting hit and hitting back harder was in the marrow of my bones. I'd tried to run away from it when I left the Navy to join the cops and do something different. But here I was going into the ring with everything on the line again.

I realized how much I'd missed it.

Trevor Haywood was big. A true light-heavy-weight. But he hadn't taken me seriously. Why should he? I was an amateur middleweight making the step up to light-heavyweight for his first pro fight. So, Haywood was big, but he was out of top shape.

When he threw a punch, I clearly saw it coming, blocking and countering. I was throwing two or three punches for every jab he threw. I felt ready. I felt strong. It was only the first round, but the fight was already taking on its unique character. It was me dancing and Haywood lumbering after me.

We were back at the Olympic Auditorium, but this time I'd been promoted to the undercard, one fight below the evening's main event. The weigh-in for the fight had been in the morning. I was still five pounds under the light-heavyweight limit, but Mama Hawks had sewn two lead weights into my silk shorts. I tipped the scales at two pounds over the lower limit.

I moved in to pound at the perceptible layer of fat around Haywood's belly. He didn't even grunt. At one time, Haywood had been a contender, but booze and broads had taken their toll. His manager had done a good job of keeping the inevitable hidden from the boxing writers, even to the point of keeping Haywood's workouts closed to reporters and the public. But, in itself, that was a bad sign, and the word was on the street.

Nothing Haywood was showing me tonight so far was going to change anything for him, even if he won.

I covered up when Haywood threw a heavy-hitting right and left. I felt the power that had once been behind them, but now they landed with more thud than bang. I kept my arms up and my elbows tucked in. I moved away, and counter punched.

The bell to end the round dinged and I headed for my corner. Pops started yammering at me while Tina took out my mouthpiece and got busy with the sponge.

When I turned my head to the right to spit, I could see Mickey Cohen and his entourage sitting in the front row. Solomon King was there as well, looking sour. It must have rankled him that if I won this fight, he'd have to fight me to get his shot.

I could also see Anita O'Shay, wrapped in a mink stole and sitting on the far side of Mickey. I could tell she was forcing herself not to look at me. Was she really into this as deep as I suspected? Or was she just another good-looking woman getting her kicks rubbing up against a big-time gangster?

"Corners out," the ref yelled.

I stood up. Tina put my mouthpiece back in. Pops was shaking his head. He knew I hadn't heard a word he'd said. I looked back down at Cohen. He wasn't looking at me. I turned to follow his gaze and saw he was looking at Tina. All the women the guy had around him, and he was looking at a thirteen-year-old kid.

The bell rang, and I turned back into the ring. Somehow, Haywood had made it across the ring and was on top of me before I realized it. He started swinging haymakers, and I was against the ropes. The crowd was cheering, egging him on to hit me and hit me. The heavy thudding blows came one after the other, battering my scrambled defense.

I rolled with the punches as best I could, catching their rhythm and sliding to the sides. A better fighter than Haywood would have finished me then and there. I'd been stupid and unprepared, but I wasn't going down, and I could feel him losing steam.

I feinted right and went left, bobbing under a lumbering right hook, and danced away to the center of the ring. Haywood turned like an angry bear. I let loose a bolo punch, looping it over his right shoulder and exploding it on the right side of his head.

The bolo was something I'd been working on

since I'd seen a film of Kid Galivan using it to take out Johnny Bratton in 1951 for the welterweight title. I liked it because it was really a distraction technique. By dropping your back hand and pretending to make an obvious wide sweeping throw, your opponent's eyes gravitated to the dropped hand, leaving you free to throw your front arm.

If you threw it enough times, your opponent would figure out what you were doing, changing his focus to your leading hand. Then you switched it up and followed through with the looping bolo punch itself. Because of the distance and torque you could put into it, it was a devastating blow when it landed.

In this instance, however, I wasn't using it as a distraction. I let loose with another bolo, from the right this time. Haywood was too shaken by the first punch to do anything to stop this one landing, and he went down to the canvas.

The ref pushed me back and away to a neutral corner. Blood was singing in my veins. This was life. I wanted Haywood to get up. I wanted to hit him again and again.

The ref ticked off five, and Haywood came up to one knee. At the eight count, he stood up. The ref rubbed Haywood's gloves off on his shirt and then moved out of the way.

"Fight," he said, signaling to me.

I moved in quickly, throwing a barrage of combinations, but Haywood was hunkered down. His thick neck had pulled his head back into his shoulders like a turtle, and he kept his thickly muscled arms up. It was a defensive posture he could cruise in all day while he got his bearings back.

The bell let loose, and I headed back to my corner. Time was funny during a match. When a fight was not going your way, the bell seemed to take three days to ring. When you were on top and banging away, three minutes seemed like three seconds.

I hated showing off, but I had a plan. As I approached my corner, I held my arms up to the crowd, who roared approval back at me. There was no feeling like it in the world.

I brought my right arm down, along with my gaze, until my fist was pointing at Solomon King. I then did a fancy little shuffle and shadow boxed back onto my stool. The crowd went crazy again. The boxing world was very small. Most everyone knew the great up and coming Solomon King, was going to have to get through me, a cocky kid putting on a show.

"What are you doing," Pops said, as I sat.

I spat out my mouthpiece. "My job," I said. "It's not about this fight; it's about the next."

"Well, you better finish this fight first, or there won't be a next."

Haywood came out for round three a lot more cautiously. The guy was a brawler, but he also had some technique. We danced and probed, neither giving or taking much punishment.

And then it happened...

Haywood accidentally on purpose stepped on my left foot with all his weight, effectively trapping me in one place and opening me up for a head butt as I tried to move away. It was a dirty trick used by desperate fighters who did it with enough skill for the ref not to notice.

What Haywood hadn't calculated was I'd been in bar fights across three continents, I'd fought on ships from here to Taiwan, and if that dirty trick had been pulled on me once, it had been pulled on me a hundred times along with a hundred others.

As soon as I felt the pressure on my foot, I moved forward instead of back. I ducked my head and bent it down. When Haywood's inevitable head butt came, instead of catching me square in the face with his forehead, he smashed the ridge of his left eyebrow into my skull. Hard.

Haywood jerked his head back in shock. As he did so, blood from the split over his eye splashed across me. His weight moved off my foot. His hands dropped momentarily in shock. And I threw a right uppercut. It started at my feet and hit him right on the point of his chin.

Haywood went straight back and down. He was out before he hit the floor.

I don't know why I felt I had to get under Solomon King's skin. Perhaps it was instinct. I'd never been in a position of knowing who my next opponent was going to be before I'd fought the previous fight.

Fighting, in war or in the ring, is as much about getting inside your opponent's head as it is about making physical contact. If I was to beat him, I needed King to think I was a fool who had gotten lucky. I needed him to underestimate me.

I was not going to underestimate him. I knew I needed every advantage I could get.

With Haywood still flat on the canvas, the ref held up my arm as the victor. I swaggered over to the ropes in front of Solomon King, Mickey Cohen, and all their cronies. I knew I was mimicking what had happened naturally after the fight with Lester Carter. Then it had been true disdain on my part. This time it was hubris.

I spat out my mouthpiece in Cohen's direction. It landed at the red stiletto-clad feet of Anita O'Shay. She was looking at me now, her expression anything but adoring.

There was no sense in pretense. Cohen knew I was the face of the police department. Chief Parker's stooge. I was being used to stop King and therefore stop Cohen from getting his claws into the fight game.

"Your boy is going down," I said to Cohen. When I said the word boy, I infused it with the intonation of every red-necked cracker I'd ever heard use the word. I was purposely avoiding talking to Solomon.

I was a little ashamed to hear myself talk in such a tone. Father Tim would have belted me one. But I was delighted by the reaction I got out of King.

Flowing to his feet, Solomon King was up and had one hand on the lowest rope, ready to pull himself into the ring, before Cohen's bodyguards could grab him from behind.

"Come on then," I said, bouncing on my toes and throwing some fast combinations. "Let's see what you've got."

I could literally hear Solomon King growling. He was like a caged panther, held back by a tether of human handlers.

I laughed and bounced away to my corner. My expression changed as soon as I saw Tombstone looking at me.

"I hope you know what you're doing," he said.

"Me too," I said. I slipped into my robe with Tina's help and slid out of the ring.

ROUND ELEVEN

"They want to move the fight up six weeks," Pops said.

"What?" I felt stunned.

"It's King's way of getting back at you for your little show at the end of the Haywood fight."

Moving the fight up six weeks only left two weeks before the big showdown. Only two months after my fight with Haywood.

I'd been concentrating on getting under King's skin. I should have been better prepared for him to counter.

"No way!" I said. "The fight date has been set. It can't be changed on a whim."

Pops sighed. "It's not a whim. It's the fight game. King's trainer, Marvin Stockbridge, says it's all set."

"We can still refuse," I said.

"If we do, it look like we be scared." This came from Tombstone in his deep basso voice.

"I need the extra time to recover from the Haywood fight," I argued.

"No, you don't," Pops said. "You came out of that fight cleaner than sparring ten rounds with Donovan, which you do every day."

"Solomon King isn't Trevor Haywood, and he sure ain't Donovan Hawks," I said. The words were out of my mouth before I realized Donovan was close enough to hear. We'd just finished sparing. His face clouded over.

"I need the time to train," I said.

"No, you don't," Pops said.

"Don't keep saying that!" I tugged helplessly at the eight-ounce glove I was trying to remove, and then tried to shake it off in frustration.

Tina Hawks moved in and grabbed my agitated hand. She made me hold still while she finished unlacing the glove. I wanted to pull my hand away from her. She was a thirteen-year-old kid, and she was in my corner going up against Solomon King. What was Chief Parker thinking?

What was I thinking?

Tina pulled the glove off. I turned and walked away before she could start to unwrap my tape. Out of the corner of my eye, I saw Pops take her shoulders and hold her back from following me.

That was fine. I didn't want anyone following me.

"Do what you want," I said over my shoulder.

It had been six weeks since the Haywood fight, and every day Pops rode me hard for calling out Solomon King like I did. I tried explaining I hadn't been showing off for the sake of showing off. I needed King overconfident if I was going to beat him. It did no good.

"Just beating King isn't going to be enough," Pops growled. "You're going to have to destroy him because he is going to be out to destroy you."

"I handled Haywood in three rounds..."

"You handled nothing!" Pops got himself into full flow. "Haywood is a has-been who never-was. You beat a strawman nothing more. Solomon King is the real deal, and he is hungry for victory. He don't care nothin' about Cohen, the mob, or your precious Chief Parker. He only cares about being the light-heavyweight champion of the world. And right now, you're standing in his way."

Every day I heard it.

And every day sparring with Donovan, I could feel Donovan holding back, smirking. He wasn't giving me his best, and he knew I knew it. He'd never come out and say it, but he wanted me to lose. Somehow, he figured he would get a shot if I went down in flames.

Tombstone wasn't any help either. He'd been

down to the Main Street Gym where King had set up camp. He'd seen King working, and he just looked at me and worried. How somebody so big could be such an old lady was beyond me.

I was so mad; I was ready to go after King right there and then. After a couple of deep breaths, I knew it was exactly what King wanted. He was getting in my head.

I wasn't ready, but I would be. Only my brother Mickey and Father Tim knew the rage down inside me. Both of them had seen it and felt it turned against them. Mickey had the same rage. Like me, he couldn't control it. On the streets, we'd almost torn the heads and limbs off kids who dared cross our paths with intent to harm. Father Tim knew he couldn't make the rage go away, but he taught us to channel and control it.

But he also taught us when and how to turn it loose.

I had no doubt Solomon King had his own rage. Once we were in the ring, it wasn't going to be about which one of us could hurt the other more. It was going to be about which one of us had been hurt the deepest. Whose rage, the ball of anger exploding in their gut, was going to engulf the other like an uncontrolled fire being consumed by a larger raging fire.

I could feel the burn starting to ignite inside of me. Maybe Pops had sensed it and was trying to bring it out. I couldn't underestimate him like I couldn't underestimate King, but it didn't matter. All I had to do was keep it under control for two more weeks.

For now, I kept walking toward the locker room, leaving the ring, and Pops, and Donovan, and Tombstone, and everything else behind me.

ROUND TWELVE

I was done training for the day. Oh, I was sure Pops wanted me to do more, watch film, talk strategy, but I was done. I was showered and putting on my clothes when Tina came into the locker room.

She was quiet, straddling the narrow wooden bench. In her dungarees and green tee shirt snitched from one of her older brothers, she looked more like eight than thirteen.

"You okay, Pat?" she asked.

I couldn't take my anger out on her. "Fine, kid," I said, my voice gentle.

"You worried about King?"

I smiled. "You worried I can't take him?"

"No way!" She was emphatic.

"All right then. Nothing to worry about. You gonna be in my corner?"

"Of course."

I finished knotting my tie and threw a couple of shadow jabs at her. "You're my good luck charm, kid. With you there, I can take this guy like a Sunday afternoon."

Tina laughed and batted at my hands. "Get outta here," she said. "I gotta clean up your mess like usual." She reached to pick my towel up off the floor.

I smiled and moved out the door.

When I got to the detective sedan, I was still focused inward. I opened the door and slid behind the wheel. It was only then I realized Tombstone was slouched down on the passenger side. His head was resting on the seat back, his hat over his eyes.

I swore.

"Give me a break. I need to get out of here. Alone." I realized I was gritting my teeth.

"You're not safe to be let out alone."

"Don't you have anywhere else to be?"

"I'm your partner," Tombstone replied simply and without heat. "You'd be sitting here if the situation were reversed."

I blew air out through my cheeks. I didn't make a move to start the car. I put my hands at ten and two on the large ceramic steering wheel and let my elbows sag.

"You don't think I can beat him, do you?"

"You seen the films," Tombstone said.

I had. Pops had scrounged up some 8mm movies of King's last two fights. Even in grainy, jerky, black and white, King was a colossus. He had two inches on me in both height and reach. His muscles were long and sinewy, making him both fast and powerful. When he hit opponents, they stayed hit. When they hit him, it made no impression.

"I've fought bigger men."

"Maybe," Tombstone said. "But have you fought tougher, smarter, faster men who know how to fight?"

I ran my left hand over my face. "Then why am I going through all this?"

"I didn't say you couldn't beat him," Tombstone said. He plucked his hat off his face and put it on his head as he sat up. He turned to face me. "But you've got to get your head right."

"What do you mean?"

"You got to forget all about Mickey Cohen, about beating King for Chief Parker, about getting on the Hat Squad. All of that is a distraction. You've got to go against King because he is standing between you and a shot at the title."

"What? I'm not going to get a title shot..."

"Not if you let King knock your brains out."

"You're crazy."

Tombstone was silent. My brain was racing.

I opened my mouth to speak, and then shut it.

Tombstone nodded. "You let me worry about

doing police work. You figure out how you gonna take King down on your route to being champin' of the world."

"Crazy..." I said softly.

Tombstone got out of the car. He walked around and opened the driver's door. "Scoot over," he said. "You too mixed up to drive."

I scooted over to the passenger side. Tombstone got in behind the wheel and turned the engine over.

"You really think I got a shot?"

He nodded. "You be where I put my money. Remember, I also seen you fight. But you can get back to working on it tomorrow. Tonight, you gonna help me do some detective work." With that, he put the car in gear and pulled into traffic.

ROUND THIRTEEN

Over an early dinner at Monty's Steakhouse on Hollywood Boulevard a couple of blocks down from Vine, Tombstone filled me in on what detective work he'd been doing while I'd been busy training.

He'd done some background work tracking Anita O'Shay back to her Kansas City roots. He'd even flown back there after telling me he needed a few days off to take care of personal business. He told me Chief Parker sponsored the trip but hadn't wanted me distracted until Tombstone came up with something concrete.

I wanted to get upset about my partner not keeping me in the mix, but he'd been right. I'd needed to keep my head in the fight game.

While he was in KC, Tombstone had come up with the goods. Anita O'Shay had been a rising star on the jazz scene in Kansas City before supposedly making her way west. The interesting thing, however, was the real Anita O'Shay was currently on an all-expense paid tour of the Havana hot spots. She hadn't come west at all.

Tombstone had dug deeper. Anita O'Shay's real name was Mary Talbot. Mary had a sister, Eve Talbot, who was a year younger. Eve not only looked and sung a lot like her sister but paid her bills by working for the Treasury Department in downtown KC. The rest of the story didn't take a lot of figuring.

"Think you're pretty good at this detective stuff," I said when we were drinking coffee with the leftover scraps from thick steaks and baked potatoes scattered around us. My voice was lightly mocking.

"About as good as you is at fighting," Tombstone said. It amused me how Tombstone slipped in and out of his poverty accent. He used it for effect, to catch people off guard and to get them to underestimate him. However, if you were a friend, he seemed to do it as if it was a joke in which he was including you. I could tell he was still feeling me out, seeing how I was going to take all this.

I raise my coffee cup to him. "Seriously," my tone was sincere, "I'm impressed. When this is over, and we're permanent on the Hat Squad, you're going to have to teach me about this detective stuff."

"Ain't much different than when you in the ring.

You tuck your chin in and keep punching."

We arrived at the Blue Cat before Eve Talbot, masquerading as her sister, Anita O'Shay, came out for her first set. I knew Louie, the guy working the door, and tipped him decent to get the right table.

The Blue Cat was a smoky little dive on the outskirts of Hollywood. It was known for hot jazz and a mixed clientele. It was sort of demilitarized zone where race didn't matter. The only requirement was you played nice and had the cash to pay the steep price for drinks.

Tombstone and I were sitting at a small table in the middle of the room. Around us at the other tables were couples and groups. Most of them were alligators—jazz fans who couldn't play an instrument but were caught by the beat of the jazz itself. Some of them, of course, only wanted to be associated with the scene. Nobody appeared to care what anybody else's reason was for being there. Most of them were well-dressed, well-heeled, and well-lubricated.

The Blue Cat had a good reputation with jazz aficionados. The seven-piece house band rotated through some of the best session players in the business. They came to the Blue Cat to jam and play, not to work. These were guys who knew every note there was and how to bring a melody back without missing a beat.

Tonight, they worked their way into the same song the sax man outside the Federal Building had been playing, Someone To Watch Over Me, and then the spot hit Miss Anita O'Shay and her voice came out rich and full of pleading. The crowd was entranced. If Eve was this good impersonating her sister, how good was the real thing? It boggled the mind.

She stood still, poured into a red sheath dress the same color as the flaming hair spilling to her shoulders. She kept it simple, not reaching for notes, no fancy vocal runs, but there was enough promise in her voice to put every man in the room under her spell. This included Mickey Cohen, who we could see sitting with three uncomfortable goons at a too small table up front.

Tombstone and I had worried about Cohen spotting us, but the gangster was too entranced to be aware of his surroundings. That was the job of his bodyguards, but even they only had eyes for the songbird on the small stage.

"If those goons don't pay better attention," I said, "Cohen could end up as dead as last year's fashions."

"Can't happen soon enough," Tombstone said.

"You think Cohen is so besotted with our Anita imposter he failed to check her out."

I could sense Tombstone shrug in the darkness. "Maybe, but her cover is pretty tight. I went looking for trouble because you spotted her at the Federal Building. I think her background would hold up to a cursory check. She's a ringer for her sister."

Anita, as I still thought of her, purred her way through a half dozen standards before taking a break. On the last number, she wandered through a couple of front tables before ending up on Mickey Cohen's lap. She gave him a quick peck on the cheek, nothing more than a show kiss, but Cohen loved the attention. He waved his hand with the fat cigar in it and made as if to grab Anita, but she deftly slipped away. She moved off the dance floor and through the curtain before the audience stopped laughing.

The band swung into an up-tempo number. It was dance music, not listening-jazz. Couples got up from their tables to fill the small dance floor.

Tombstone and I got up, but not to dance. At least not in the literal sense. The doorman, Louie, was now acting as a backstage bouncer, but he let us slide past without comment.

Behind the scenes, The Blue Cat was stripped down. What money the club earned was spent out front for the customers. In the back, there was a threadbare carpet leading down a short hallway to a couple of dressing rooms.

The door of the first was open. I tapped on it and stepped in when I saw Anita sitting in front of a lighted mirror. She was checking her makeup and turned with a big smile. It disappeared as soon as she saw me.

"What are you doing here?"

"Hello to you too," I said. I knew Tombstone would be in the hallway covering my back.

Anita stood up, calling out, "Louie!"

"Take it easy, Eve," I said. It stopped her cold. "We're on the same side."

"If Mickey catches you back here, he'll hurt both of us. You've got him all riled up over this fight with Solomon." Her eyes flashed with both challenge and fear.

"I'm sure you're stoking his fire every chance you get to keep him away from finding out what you're really doing."

"And what am I really doing? And my name is Anita, not Eve."

"You're way too late for bluster." I laughed softly. "How are you going to survive as a Treasury agent if this is how you maintain your cover."

She sat down again, defeated. "I'm not an agent," she said, almost in a whisper. "I was a secretary. I was recruited for this job because my boss saw me sing one evening in KC when my sister was sick. He felt it could be the perfect cover."

"It could get you perfectly dead if Mickey Cohen finds out. And how come KC is sending somebody undercover in L.A.?"

"If you know what I'm doing, then you know I'm chasing Verne Chadwick. His first turn as a counterfeiter was in Kansas City. It's KC's case."

"You found what sweatshop is hiding the printing press yet?"

She stood up, seeming to get some of her confidence back. "You are a bright boy. I haven't found it yet, but I will."

There was a commotion in the hallway. I talked fast and low. "If we can find out who you are, Cohen can find out who you are. Keep your head down and don't give him a reason to go looking."

"Thanks for nothing," she said. "I've got another set." She pushed me aside and went out the door. "Mickey, baby!" she said, sounding delighted as she entered the hall. "I wondered where you were."

"Sorry, sir," I heard a voice say. It could only belong to Tombstone, but it was flat and nowhere near as deep as usual. "I didn't know the lady knew you."

I stayed in the room listening. Eve as Anita played her part perfectly. "I'm sorry, Mickey. I forgot to tell the new guy to let you through."

"Yeah," Cohen said. "I don't care how big he is or good at bouncing. I want Louie to fire the guy now."

"Okay, baby," Anita said. As her voice was fading, it was clear she was guiding Cohen away.

A few seconds later, Tombstone stuck his head in the door. "Looks like I'm gonna be fired," he said in with his normal resonance.

I shook my head. "It's a tough town."

ROUND FOURTEEN

The next day, it was back to the grind. Or at least it's what I thought. The night before had been little more than a jape. It was validation for Tombstone's efforts in confirming my hunch about Anita O'Shay. The city cops had let the feds know they weren't as smart as the thought. It had been a game of tit-for-tat, which could have turned out nasty. Fortunately, the back hallway had been too dark for Cohen to recognize Tombstone and maybe force a standoff with his hoods. And just as fortunately, Cohen didn't walk in while I was talking to Eve.

The implications of what Tombstone had said earlier in the evening had started me thinking about a title shot beyond fighting Solomon King. I was fired up and full of energy. It gave me part of the mental edge I'd been missing.

The physical edge I'd been missing walked into Ten Hawks Gym as I was getting ready to spar with Donovan. It was Willy Stevenson and his trainer,

Buddy Doyle. If King got past me, Stevenson was the final fighter he'd have to face before getting a championship shot at Archie Moore.

Stevenson climbed into the ring. Buddy Doyle had pulled Willy's robe off, and underneath he was already dressed for action. Like Solomon King, Willy was two inches taller than me and built solid. The few years he had on me could be seen in the lines of his face, but nowhere else. "I hear you're playing policeman for me," he said, using the term in the boxing sense—a protector. "Gonna keep Solomon King from getting to me."

Already in the ring, Donovan didn't like being cut out of the picture. The arrogance he displayed with me was even more clearly displayed toward Willy. I'd talked to Pops about it, but he had just shrugged. Donovan was his oldest. He loved him, but like a lot of parents, he couldn't get through to him.

"Get out of here, kid," Willy said to Donovan, dismissing him without even looking at him. "The men have work to do."

Willy touched gloves with me, and we started circling. We threw some half-speed stuff. Nothing of consequence, just warming up.

"King has got two inches in height on you," Willy said. "Like me. It means our reach is longer as well."

We were throwing punches faster now, getting warmer.

"Always keep the pressure on a taller man," Willy said. "You want to get inside, so you have to move forward." He shuffled forward, forcing me back. I didn't like it, but I didn't have a choice. "Big guys often have coordination problems. They're not as agile as smaller fighters."

Willy kept coming at me. We were almost up to full speed. I was purposely blocking and slipping only. Willy didn't have a mouthpiece in, and I needed to hear what he was telling me.

"If you keep him moving backwards, the odds are he'll be out of his comfort zone," Willy continued. "Lots of tall fighters need to get set to punch. Don't give him the moment he needs to set his punches." Willy's movements in the ring showed me what he was talking about even more than his words.

"The best way to neutralize his reach advantage is to fight inside. When you're in close, you're not in danger from his long-range straight right. Work on your uppercuts to the body and your hooks." Willy threw those punches, and I did my best to roll with them.

"When he throws a punch, you throw a flurry of punches. Never try to potshot him with only one punch. Always string your punches together in combination. You can't hit him if you don't throw punches."

Willy backed off. "Buddy," he said.

Doyle climbed into the ring.

"Okay," Willy said, right before Doyle slipped his mouthpiece in. "Let's see what you got."

The rest of the week continued the same way. Every day, Willy came to spar with me in the ring.

"You've seen it in the films," Willy told me as he acted out the part of Solomon King. "He's lazy about bringing his jab back, so you've got to counterpunch him."

Willy pulled his jab back in the same motion I'd seen Solomon King do when I watched the films over and over. I flashed into counterpunch, forcing Willy to cover up and move backward.

"Good! Good!" Pops encouraged from the corner. "You've got to make him afraid to commit to the jab. Keep parrying the jab."

"If he over-commits and jumps in with it, you give him a feint." Wily again acted out what he was telling me. "Making him throw the jab gives you an instant to step past his outstretched lead hand and throw a hook to his body."

I followed the instructions and punched through. We did it over and over and over.

Afterward, leaning on the ropes together, Willy

kept talking. "The problem you're going to have is it will be difficult to actually hit King with the overhand right early in a fight because you're really using it as a distraction. You have to set it up by getting him accustomed to your left hook. From King's point of view, your overhand right has got to look like the initial part of your left hook. It's only a deceptive and deadly punch when he's expecting the left hook."

Every day, I learned more. Every day, Pops and Willy kept at me. I was exhausted at first, but as the days wore on, I felt stronger and stronger.

Monday afternoon before the fight on the coming Saturday, the first disaster struck.

Pops had been winding down the hard workouts. Everything now was about maintaining speed and staying sharp. The mood in Ten Hawks was positive. Pops had let the reporters in the prior Friday, and the boxing writers had been doing their job pumping up the fight on the sports pages. My performance against Haywood had them all buzzing.

Despite Solomon King's record of devastating opponents, all the articles were being written as if I was going to be a match for him. At least all the articles Tombstone read to me. I knew there would be naysayers, but he wasn't going to read those, and I didn't want to hear them.

I was untaping my hands when Tina came running into the gym. "Pops! Pops!" She was highly agitated.

We all looked over at her.

"What is it?" Pops asked, concerned.

"It's Donovan," she was out of breath from running. "He went over to Main Street to spar with King, and he's getting killed."

There was a moment when nobody moved, then Tombstone and I were running out to the detective sedan.

The Main Street Gym was on the second floor at 318½ Main, above a luggage store and a parking garage. A sign above the ground floor entry read, World ranked boxers train here daily. From the outside, it looked rundown, but inside it was all business with six solid rings set up for training and all the equipment anyone could need.

I had the tape off my hands by the time Tombstone drove the six blocks from Ten Hawks to Main Street Gym. He screeched to a halt at the curb on the wrong side of the street. We were out of the car and running toward the entrance before the sedan's springs stopped rocking.

Bursting into the gym, we could see a large crowd hooting and hollering. With Tombstone leading the charge, we started plowing through people until we could get to ringside.

It was an awful sight.

Solomon King had beaten Donovan Hawks sil-ly. He'd done it in such a way as to keep Donovan barely on his feet. His face without headgear was a bruised, bloodied, pulpy mess. Donovan could barely get his hands up above his waist.

When he saw me coming, King punched Dono-van with a straight right to the head. The force of the punch sent Donovan into the ropes and then springing him back into a left-right combination, finally putting him on the floor—either out or dead.

King was slick with sweat. He spat out his mouth-piece. "Come on, boy," he said, waving me toward him with his gloves. His voice was surprisingly high, so different than the threatening presence his body projected, so different from Tombstone's deep basso, which was what I thought should have been coming out of his mouth.

It was this incongruity more than anything else that stopped me from seeing red. Donovan was an arrogant kid, but he had a great future ahead of him with time to mature, if this hadn't killed him or broken his will.

Donovan was young and immature. He thought he was invincible. He was jealous because he didn't want to wait for his shot. The Golden Gloves, The Olympics, they were his path to the top, but he hadn't wanted to wait. He thought he was ready. He thought he could beat me. He thought he could beat King. He was wrong. He was almost dead wrong.

I felt the rage deep inside me, but it was rage at myself. My arrogant goading of King had caused him to dupe and beat Donovan. I thought I was getting into his mind, but he had turned it all back on me. I was into the ring, but I was icy enough to kneel next to Donovan, and not go after King. The crowd had gone silent. The mob mentality which had urged them on to jeer and cheer had fled. The only thing left behind was their shame.

And mine.

Then Tombstone was beside me as I cradled Donovan's head.

"Ambulance is coming," he said, and I could hear the wail of the siren in the distance.

I looked up at King, who was still standing, smirking. I looked over at his trainer Marvin Stockbridge, who couldn't hold my gaze. There were various hoods connected to Mickey Cohen outside the ring, but the big man himself was no-where to be seen. He had let this happen, but he wouldn't want to be directly connected to it.

However, for me, this wasn't about Cohen any-more. This was about me and King. And there was a war coming.

ROUND FIFTEEN

The next few days before the fight went by in a concentrated blur. I was turned almost completely inward. I spoke only when spoken to directly, and only then in one or two-word answers.

Donovan was stabilized, but still in a light coma. He had come out of it once but retreated back in again. It felt as if I were encased in ice, yet with a fire so hot at my center, it felt as if it were consuming me.

Every day, I was readying myself mentally for the ring. Solomon King had misjudged me badly. He sought to intimidate me, to make me fear him. But I felt no fear; I never had. I did feel hate.

In the crucible of the ring, I was going to destroy Solomon King. I was Patrick Felony Flynn, and I was a giant killer.

And then the world exploded.

It was late. I was in my room above Ten Hawks Gym, lying on my bed fully clothed except for my shoes. I wanted to sleep, but Morpheus wouldn't come. Whenever I closed my eyes, I saw King's fists pounding into Donovan. I'd been through enough close calls to know I wasn't invincible, but I knew I could beat King. I would beat King.

I heard the phone ringing in the hallway. It rang three times before somebody answered it. A few moments later, there was a knock on my door. Tina came in.

"Pat, that was Donovan's nurse. He's awake and calling for you. They say he wouldn't calm down unless somebody called you."

I sat up on the bed and began putting on my shoes. "Call Tombstone," I said.

"I will," Tina said, "But I'm going with you."

I couldn't refuse her. She'd been staying by her brother's side more than anyone else. She'd earned the right to go.

Tombstone was at the hospital when we arrived. Our badges got us past the night nurse, but she insisted Tina stay in the visitor's waiting room. I quietly promised Tina I'd get her in to see Donovan before we left.

There was another nurse in Donovan's room. She looked up when we came in. "Are you Patrick Flynn?"

"Yes, ma'am," I said.

"He's been insisting on talking with you. The doctor only agreed because it appears to be the only way to get him to calm down."

I moved past her to the bed. Donovan's eyes opened. The bruising on his face was changing color as it healed. The swelling was way down.

He reached out and grabbed my arm.

"I'm sorry, Pat." His voice was soft and sand dry.

I helped him drink some water through a straw.

"There's nothing to be sorry for," I told him.

"Yes," he insisted. "They were here right after I woke up."

"Who was here?"

"Two men."

"Doctors?"

"No! No!" He was getting upset.

"Easy," I said. "Tell it slow."

"They were thugs."

I looked over at Tombstone.

"Somebody on the hospital staff must have let them know he was awake," he said.

I turned back to Donovan. "What did they want?"

There was sweat on Donovan's forehead. "They said you have to lose."

I shook my head. "They're just trying to scare us."

"No!" Donovan was insistent. His hand dug into

my arm. "They said they were going to take Tina until after the fight."

"That's crazy. Tina is with us..." My voice trailed off.

Tombstone was out of the room before me.

The waiting room was empty.

The bathroom was empty.

The hallways were empty.

We ran outside, but the parking lot was empty.

Tina was gone.

"They must have been waiting for us to bring her here," Tombstone said.

"Either that or they had the gym staked out and were planning to take her when we were out of the way," I said, my stomach jumping in all directions.

"Guess it don't make no difference," Tombstone said. "She's gone."

"And Mickey Cohen has her," I said, finishing the horror for both of us.

ROUND SIXTEEN

Three hours before the fight, we were still no closer to finding Tina than we were at the hospital the night before. I felt sick. Tombstone and I had been so foolish when we started this in thinking Mickey Cohen couldn't get to us.

We might not have had wives or girlfriends or blood family he could reach, but everybody has somebody or something they care about. Ugly men like Mickey Cohen knew that and had no compunction about exploiting the knowledge.

I was alone in the main dressing room at the Olympic Auditorium. I'd chased everyone else out. I wasn't fit company to be around. I was here because I couldn't think of anywhere else to go. Others were still heavily involved in the search for Tina. Chief Parker had mobilized all his available assets, but to no avail.

Every known Cohen gunsel had been hauled in and either sweated, bribed, or beaten, but to a man, they knew nothing. Street snitches who would sell out their mother for a sawbuck could come up with nothing but wild goose chases.

Trying to postpone the fight would have sealed Tina's death warrant the same as if I refused to take a dive and go in the tank.

The tension at the weigh-in earlier in the day had been palpable. I made weight by two pounds without the aid of Pops' lead-lined shorts.

King and I simply stared at one another. He had two inches on me in height and outweighed me by ten pounds, but stripped down, muscle for muscle, we looked evenly matched.

I knew the serious training and proper nutrition had changed my body into a brawny, twisted steel sinew of fast, fighting muscle. I felt the power inside me. I'd never before been in this kind of shape. Physically, I felt ready. I was packed, tamped, and ready to ignite. Mentally, I was a mass of confusion.

I was scared I was going to lose control in the ring, forget what was at stake, forget to go down, and destroy King. I knew it could happen. I'd seen red and lost all control before. I was Patrick Felony Flynn the giant killer because I never stopped coming, I couldn't stop coming, I'd be throwing fists from my grave. But if I couldn't stop myself, how could I go down?

King vs. Flynn was at the top of tonight's fight card. The main event. The boxing writers had been spinning the fight up in the local sports pages, so the audience was expected to be large and frenzied. Word of what King had done to Donovan had spread through the boxing community like a plague, turning what would have been a fairly standard match-up into a grudge match.

It was what Cohen wanted. If King got past me, Willy Stevenson couldn't dodge him any longer. And King would go through Stevenson and get his shot at Archie Moore and the World Light-Heavyweight Championship. Once King put the belt in Cohen's pocket, there would be no stopping Cohen from taking over the rest of the fight game. It would turn a sport already battling accusations of fixing and dirty dealings into a deadly business.

And because Cohen had Tina, I could do nothing to stop it.

The door to the dressing room opened, and Tombstone stepped in. I looked up sharply, but the expression on his face was enough to tell me there was no good news.

"How you doing?" he asked.

I blew out a long breath and went back to pacing. I shook my head but didn't say anything.

"We'll find her," Tombstone said.

I stopped and looked over at him. "No, we won't. In real life, sometimes the bad guys win."

"Since when?" Tombstone was trying, but I wasn't buying.

"This whole plan was a bad idea. Whatever made anyone think I could take down King? I was crazy to take this on."

It was Tombstone's turn to shake his head. "That's your black cloud talking. If this hadn't happened, if you could fight King toe to toe, you could take him."

"But this has happened," I said. "Donovan is in the hospital. Tina is gone. All because we were arrogant."

"This is not our fault. This situation is because of Mickey Cohen. His choices, not ours."

"If Tina doesn't come back alive, does it make any difference whose choice it was?"

"Yes," Tombstone said. His tone had changed, and I looked up to see vengeance in his eyes.

We stared at each other, a silent pact being made.

The door to the dressing room opened again, noise from the auditorium louder now than when Tombstone entered. We looked up, expecting to see Pops, and got a big surprise.

Eve Talbot, aka Anita O'Shay, undercover Treasury agent.

She looked upset and emotionally torn. "I know where she is." The words came out in a rush, tumbling over themselves and running together as if she wouldn't say them if she didn't get them out fast enough.

Both Tombstone and I looked at her silently. Her words were a shock, but knowing she was a Treasury agent was even more disorienting.

"What do you mean?" I asked. It was a stupid question. She couldn't mean anyone else other than Tina, but I didn't want to get my hopes up by jumping to conclusions.

"The little girl, Tina, of course."

"Where is she?" Tombstone asked. His whole body was a study in controlled fury.

"Cohen stashed her in the garment district with Verne Chadwick. Cohen has kept the location of this whole counterfeiting operation under heavy wraps except for a very few trusted lieutenants. I overheard them talking when they thought I'd left the room."

"Why are you telling us and not your boss?" I asked.

"I did tell my boss, but he won't move on Cohen."

"What!" Tombstone and I said in unison.

Anita shook her head. "He doesn't care about your fight, and he doesn't think Cohen will kill the girl. We know the counterfeiting operation can't roll until a load of paper stolen from the mint arrives. My boss wants it all—the plates, the presses, the paper, and Verne Chadwick."

"And he'd let Cohen keep a kidnapped girl?"

"As I said, he doesn't think Cohen will kill her. Says it would be bad for business."

"Then why are you here?" It was Tombstone's turn to ask.

"Because I believe Cohen will kill the girl. I've spent enough time with him to know he'll kill her even if you lose the fight. If anyone gets in his way, he makes them pay, and you're in his way."

"So, give already," I demanded.

ROUND SEVENTEEN

King hit me with a straight right I saw coming from down the street. The fact I saw it coming and could have blocked it didn't make the force of it any less when it hit me.

The fanfare and the fight had started on time. The Olympic Auditorium was throbbing with fans and the night was alive with anticipation.

The undercard attraction had been a blood-fest with two popular Mexican lightweights repeatedly and illegally raking the laces of their gloves across each other's faces. Nothing was settled between the two fighters, other than to increase their animosity toward each other. The fight had ended in a split decision, which guaranteed a rematch.

The fans had loved it and wanted more.

By the time I appeared as the challenger in the main event, followed into the ring two minutes later by King, the crowd was already howling for more blood. They fed on the violence and expected it from the start.

King followed the straight right with a left jab. He should have followed it with a knockout blow, but it was as if he was surprised he'd hit me so easily. Sweat ran into my eyes, so I wasn't sure, but I thought there was confusion on King's features.

The bell rang to end the first round. The crowd booed. They expected, demanded, more.

I went back to my corner and plunked down on the stool. Pops was in front of me, but there was no Tina to squeeze a sponge of cold water across my neck and down my back.

"I'm sorry. I'm sorry," Pops kept repeating as he worked on me. The strain in his face was awful.

"Stop apologizing, Pops," I said. "It's my fault, not yours. I have to take my medicine."

"Don't let him hit you like that again," Pops said. "You've got too hard a head. You won't go down that way unless he kills you."

"What am I supposed to do, Pops? I have no choice, but to let him hit me."

"Make a fight of it!" Pops demanded. "There is still time."

I simply grunted and sucked my mouthpiece into place.

"Corners out," the ref yelled, and the bell for the second round rang.

Anita had given Tombstone the address of a sweatshop hidden deep in the garment district. It was where she believed Cohen had stashed both Tina and Verne Chadwick's counterfeiting operation.

Anita and Tombstone had fled the dressing room at top speed, Tombstone to call in the rest of The Hat Squad, and Anita to return to her role on Cohen's arm.

From the ring, before the start of the fight, I'd looked down to see Anita sitting next to Cohen. I knew Cohen had a wife, but she apparently never appeared in public. I wondered if it was her choice or Cohen's.

Anita looked very pale. How she could even be near the man was beyond me. I understood if she had disappeared, Cohen would have known something was up, but her proximity to him still bothered me. It just wasn't safe.

Coming out for round two, King appeared tentative. He was feeling me out. He threw some punches, but there was no snap to them. He was giving me openings, and when I didn't take them, he stepped back. We were circling each other like a couple of little old ladies.

The crowd didn't like it and was heatedly vocalizing its displeasure. After the blood and violence of the previous fight, King and I were a huge let down so far.

And then it dawned on me. King didn't know about Tina.

Could he really be so naïve?

King allowed me to put him on the ropes. I couldn't help myself. It was instinct. He was giving me the shots, but even though he was on the defensive, he was manipulating me. He pushed off the ropes with his back and grabbed me in a clinch.

"Why aren't you fighting?" His high voice was garbled by his mouthpiece, but I understood him. Away from my ear, his words would be lost in the crowd noise.

"Your boss is holding my trainer's daughter," I mumbled back.

We broke, flashing punches at each other, which looked harder and faster than they were.

King came straight at me. We exchanged flurries, and it was my turn to clinch.

"You didn't know?"

"Hell no! I can take you fair."

We danced around. The ref slapped me on the back and yelled, "Break!"

"Tombstone has gone to get her," I said in King's ear. "Let's make this look good till then."

We parted, and King tagged me with a right uppercut as I moved away. I hadn't meant that good.

The bell rang to end the round, and we retreated to our corners.

"What's going on?" Pops asked, wiping me down.

"Any sign of them?" I asked, ignoring Pops. I looked around but could see nothing in the crowd.

Tombstone had been gone for more than two hours. If Tina had been where Anita said, then he should be back by now. Unless the news was bad.

In the third round, King and I picked up the pace. It was still a sparring match, but there was a sting in our punches and we moved good. I ridiculously found myself enjoying the confrontation. King was an excellent fighter, with amazing control and reactions. Moving around each other, looking for openings, testing, countering, attacking defending, moving, always moving. It was a ballet of sorts. A choreography of sweat and punches as precise and demanding as a dance could be in which two men were trying to destroy each other.

But we weren't.

Not yet.

The fight was now an exhibition of skill. How long we could carry it, I didn't know.

"Patrick! Patrick! Patrick!" The voice rose above the crowd, penetrated the intense concentration of the fight.

"Patrick! Patrick!"

I rolled with a punch, moved to the side, threw a three-punch combination to move King back, and took one second to look to my left, to where the voice was continuing to yell my name.

And there Tina was, sitting on Tombstone's shoulders as he strode down the aisle.

Ten hard men, all wearing sharp suits with Fedoras or Borsalinos, followed behind carrying axe handles. It was The Hat Squad, with Chief Parker at the forefront in full uniform.

As the bell to end the third round sounded, The Hat Squad moved in to surround Cohen and his bodyguards. They took no immediate action, beyond cutting Anita/Eve out of the pack to take her into protective custody. Then they simply allowed their presence to speak for itself.

ROUND EIGHTEEN

From the bell starting the fourth round, the fight turned into a war. The bell seemed to sound higher and sharper, like the report from a starter's pistol at a track meet.

King and I met in the center of the ring like two opposing freight trains. We were all out, fists flying, no covering up, toe to toe, battering and being battered. The crowd roared.

The blood sung through my veins, every muscle engorged and alive. I felt the thuds of King's fists, but there was no pain, only a strange kind of beauty. This fight, this round, this moment, this now, was the culmination of everything in my life. There was nothing outside of the ring, nothing beyond the violent embrace of King's fist and my answering responses.

Something had happened inside me when it was apparent King had no idea about the kidnap. Suddenly, I saw his honor. He was a fighter. Proud and angry, even perhaps hate-filled, but he was a fighter, a true man who lived and died by the law of the fist.

And so was I.

I was Patrick Felony Flynn, the giant killer, and I lived to match my heart, my skill, and my very soul against other men of the same creed.

Solomon King was such a man.

King's relentless fists drove me slowly backward. I answered every punch from him with one of my own. I sidestepped and slipped a strong straight right, throwing a looping left of my own into King's exposed torso. He grunted, smashing me with a clubbed left to my right shoulder. Numbness tingled for a split second down my arm.

I jabbed with my left, once, twice, three times. I was moving King backward, trying to remember all the things Willy Stevenson had drilled into me.

The heat in my brain cooled enough for me to start thinking, to start responding instead of re-acting to King's assault. I started feinting with my rights and throwing my left like Willy taught me.

King threw a triple combination toward my head. I parried the first and slipped the second, but the third caught me hard. On instinct, I pushed forward instead of backing up. I stepped inside the start of King's follow-up right hook and drove my own a left jab into his heart.

My shot should have stopped him cold, but King's right hook had been a feint, and the power of my punch to his heart was tempered by my walking into a solid shot from King's deadly left fist to my chin.

Both of us swayed apart and away. I stumbled but kept my feet. King also staggered two steps backward. The crowd shot to its feet, roaring, yelling for one or the other of us to go down.

I lurched back toward King. He lurched toward me. We exchanged blows, grunting with effort.

The bell rang.

Neither King nor or I were aware of it. We kept throwing punches, trying to smash each other, two mountains of granite with sledgehammers for arms.

Then the referee was between us, the bell ringing again and again. Pops and King's trainer, Stockbridge, were pulling us apart.

We separated, literally dragged to our corners. I was crazed. I wouldn't sit on the stool. I bounced from one foot to the other, not even aware of Tina trying to sponge me down. The second I'd seen her safe, every sense of dread in my brain had been swept away by the fury bursting inside me.

I was ignoring Pops, trying to look around him

at King, who was standing in his own corner trying to look at me. Pops instructions and pleadings were lost in the sound of the crowd, which had become a palpable physical presence.

Pops was barely able to get out of my way when the bell rang. I was across the ring, three-quarters of the way to King's corner when I met him in a crash. We bounced, clinched, and lost our balance. Both of us fell to the canvas more wrestlers than boxers.

We came up together, ready to tear into each other, but the referee got between us again. He tried cooling us down with a standing eight count, then rubbed our gloves off on his shirt before turning us loose again. It didn't slow us down.

I moved in, trying to get inside King's reach. I hammered at his body, leaving purplish welts glowing on his black skin with every blow. My gloves felt as hot as if my fists were on fire.

For his part, King was clouting my ears and kidneys, repeatedly clubbing me with his fourteen-inch fist as if he were a blacksmith trying to forge iron.

I threw a looping left I thought was going to hit home. However, King jerked his head forward at the last split second, taking the punch high on his forehead where it did little damage.

The barrage of flying leather continued through the sixth and the seventh.

Before the start of the eighth, Pops' words finally got through to me.

"You've got to hit him from the canvas like I taught ya.' If you don't, he ain't never going down, and you're gonna lose this in a split decision. Ya' know Cohen has got the judges rigged. Ya' got to put him down."

I could feel the swelling on my cheeks and around my eyes, but I could still see pretty good. My nose was mashed, but I hadn't breathed through it in years, so it didn't make no never mind.

What was important was I could still feel a spring in my legs and my arms felt strong. I felt well oiled, all my parts in working order. The damage was superficial welts and bruises, but nothing had gone bone deep.

I was ravenous to fight.

King was bigger, heavier, had a longer reach, and was in tremendous physical shape. But, I was far from done.

On ships and on land, in bars and alleys, in smokers and VFW halls, I'd fought men who were bigger and badder than me. I'd faced down enemies in three-quarters of the world. And I'd never run out of heart. What I had to find out now was how much heart King had left in him.

If there was one thing I'd learned from all the fights, against all the odds, was the man who keeps on slugging, who keeps on coming, who doesn't flinch, is the man who wins the fight.

The bell rang to start the eighth, and I took the fight to King, slugging and coming on and on. I brushed aside a pair of snapping jabs and slipped inside to punish King's body. I kept slamming away until I had him on the ropes.

He refused to go down, slipping away and stinging me hard on the left side under my kidney.

I growled in pain, an angry bear, and chased after him. I was on the edge of control, a red glow slipping down inside my eyeballs. I gave no thought to defense, only all-out assault.

King bobbed and weaved, trying to dance away, but instinctively, I was aware his legs had slowed down, his footwork sluggish. So, I hit him again and again.

And then the moment came.

King was tired, and it showed in the lazy way he pulled his arm back to start a jab. It was the same movement I'd seen again and again in the films I'd watched. He'd broken the habit for most of the fight, but he was tired, and there it was.

I started to throw my left, as I had done the whole

fight. King saw it coming and over-committed to his jab, thinking he'd slip the left and I'd be open for him to stun me with his right.

As he threw the jab, I moved away from my feinting left, stepped inside King's deadly jab, and threw an overhand right.

But I didn't just throw the right; I launched it.

I finally knew what Pops' had been preaching about. For the first time, I felt the detonation of power from the canvas under my right foot flow up my leg, though my torso, into my shoulder, down my arm, and explode out my fist as I connected with King's chin.

He hung on the end of my fist for an instant before the follow through of the punch lifted him off his feet and dropped him flat on the canvas.

His already limp, unconscious, body bounced once, flopping his arms out to either side, and then King was still.

My own head exploded with noise as the focus of the fight vanished and the world crashed down around me. The crowd was on its feet, screaming. The Hat Squad was scaring the heck out of everyone around them as they banged their axe handles on the seats in approval.

Cohen and his bodyguards were trying to slip away. One of the lugs reached for Anita and instantly got an axe handle across his shoulders for his trouble.

Then I felt Tina's young arms wrap around me, followed by Tombstone embracing both of us at the same time. Pops was there too, yelling something I couldn't hear.

I freed myself and moved to where Marvin Stockbridge was waving smelling salts under King's nose. The fighter's head moved away from the smell, his eyes opening. He was groggy but appeared okay. Stockbridge and another cornerman helped King to his feet.

King looked at me out of swelling eyes and nodded twice.

I nodded back.

I was Patrick Felony Flynn, the giant killer.

EPILOGUE

I was alone in my room above Ten Hawks Gym again. I couldn't sleep. I couldn't even sit still. I bounced on the bed for a few seconds, then got up and paced the small space.

Earlier, Tombstone had told me how he and the rest of The Hat Squad had torn apart the garment district until they got to the sweatshop where Anita had said Tina was being kept along with Verne Chadwick and his counterfeiting operation. They had found everything, even the stolen paper, which had just been delivered. It was going to be almost impossible to tie the operation back to Cohen, but it was going to hurt his organized crime machine like nothing else.

Anita was already heading back to Kansas and from there to another undisclosed city for her own protection. She was a good kid, and I would have like to have seen more of her, but some things weren't meant to be.

Chief Parker was riding high on the publicity from the arrest. He'd already told us we were fully fledged Hat Squad members from here on out.

As I paced, I relived the fight in my mind over and over.

There was a knock on my door.

I really didn't want company. I'd spent time with everyone after the fight. Now, all I wanted was to be alone and quiet. It was why I was up in my room instead of downstairs in the gym where everyone was still celebrating.

"Open up," Tombstone said from the other side of the door. "You're gonna want to see this."

I opened the door.

"This just came." Tombstone handed me an envelope. "Hand delivered."

It went through my mind it might be a death threat from Cohen, but then I saw the handwriting and disregarded that thought for another day.

The note was from Willy Stevenson.

Archie says you deserve a shot at the title, but you're going to have to get through me first. And remember, I know everything about you. See you in the ring in twelve weeks.

I showed the note to Tombstone.

I was Patrick Felony Flynn, the giant killer, and I was going to get my shot...

II. FIGHTCARD: SWAMP WALLOPER

ROUND ONE

LOS ANGELES, 1955

I was stalking Willy Stevenson around the ring as if he were a bull elephant and I was a great white hunter. We were five rounds into a scheduled ten rounder, but I knew the longer we fought, the more the odds were on a decision going Stevenson's way.

This was Madison Square Garden. A far cry from the Los Angeles Olympic Auditorium, where I'd once appeared in off the card amateur bouts. The arena was heaving with fans. They'd waited all night for this fight and were getting restless with the lack of action, let alone blood.

Willy had two inches on me in height and a couple of years in age. The biggest difference, however, was his pro light-heavyweight record of twenty-six wins and one loss. Twenty of those wins were by knockout. His one loss was to the light-heavyweight champion of the world, Archie Moore.

My biggest fight as a pro had been my first. A knockout of top light-heavyweight contender Solomon King. It was a fight for which Willy Stevenson had helped me prepare. Since then, I'd also punched out a couple of pro *tomato cans* catching the last train to Palookaville. Those fights hadn't been fixed, but they had been cosmetic.

I'd been expected to win.

Boxing tradition needed to be observed. I couldn't go straight from my first pro fight, defeating Solomon King, to a shot at Willy. There were too many other contenders and their managers who would have conniption-fitted themselves into traction. The way I defeated Solomon King might have earned me a shot at Willy, and if I got past him, a shot at Archie Moore. But I'd also had to earn a few more stripes to make the matchup with Willy legit.

At this point, I wished there had been a couple more preparation bouts. Willy was the real deal. He was smart, in shape, proud, and determined. He had never gone down easy, and he wasn't about to lay down for a young pup like me.

Since the start of the fight, I'd been trying to

move in on Willy, force him to back-pedal and lose his reach advantage. But instead of moving back, he kept moving smoothly to the side, letting loose with iron-fisted jabs. I slipped most of the shots with my forearms, but the heavy punches were taking their toll. Willy was scoring points, and I was getting frustrated.

My previous fight against Solomon King had been a crowd pleaser. However, there had been a lot more riding on the outcome than the punch jockey standings. When I wasn't slinging punches in the ring, I was trading them with hoods in the back alleys of Los Angeles' toughest neighborhoods. My career as a pro fighter had started as the result of my profession as a newly promoted detective with the Los Angeles Police Department.

Because of my boxing history while assigned to the U.S. Navy's Shore Patrol, which had taken me through every dive bar in the South Pacific, LAPD's Chief Parker had picked me to stop organized crime gangster Mickey Cohen from getting his hooks into the fight game. By taking down Cohen's fighter, Solomon King, I'd not only secured my detective promotion, and an assignment to Chief Parker's handpicked *Hat Squad*, but also earned a shot at fighting Willy Stevenson, who was a *policeman* of a different type.

In boxing parlance, a *policeman* is a fighter who protects the current champion from having to face every contender who thinks he deserves a shot. Willy Stevenson had gone down to a monstrous right cross in the final round in his loss to Archie Moore. Now, he was the man every legitimate up-and-coming fighter had to go through before they could get a shot at Moore's title belt. In the past year, nobody had proven good enough to beat Willy. It had made it easy for Moore to spend his time punching out a couple of set-ups to keep his hand in.

I'd been promised a legitimate shot at Moore if I could get past Willy, but that was proving to be a huge obstacle. When the timekeeper rang the bell to end the round, Willy immediately disengaged and moved to his corner. He didn't make eye contact or even acknowledge I was in the ring with him.

Back in my own corner, I plopped down on the low stool and spat my mouthpiece into Pop Hawks' waiting hand. Pops had been my trainer while I was an amateur and now as a pro. He was a retired L.A. cop who owned Ten Hawks Gym, named for Pops' extended brood of ten natural and adopted kids. It was located a block away from LAPD's Central station where I'd once been assigned. The gym was still where I hung up my gloves at night, living in two rooms on the second floor.

"You ain't getting it done out there," Pops said. He poured water into my mouth. I swirled it around and spat it into a bucket held by Tina Hawks, Pops' teenage tomboy daughter.

"Ain't no judges going to give you a decision," Pops continued, rubbing Vaseline over my eyebrows and the skin above.

"Tell me something I don't know," I said in-between rasping breaths. I stood up. "He knows everything I'm going to do."

"Then do something he doesn't know," Pops said. He slipped my mouthpiece back in and climbed out of the ring, taking my stool with him just as the bell sounded to start the next round.

Willy came out to meet me as he had done every round, confident and unhurried. We traded a couple of desultory jabs, and the crowd began to boo and catcall.

With those first lackluster exchanges, I realized what my problem was—I liked Willy. In past fights, both in the ring and out, I'd had no connection to my opponent. Against Solomon King, I'd had a deep burning anger and a job to do. Against Willy, I had none of those things.

And then he hit me. Hard. Rocking my head back.

The shots we'd traded earlier in the fight were taps by comparison. My body turned instinctively to ride the power from the punch and rolled into another bomb from Willy's right hand.

I staggered back, but Willy gave me no reprieve. He crowded in, forcing me back against the ropes. As I moved my hands up to cover my head, Willy let loose on my body. I tucked my elbows in, trying to protect my ribs, but the move opened my jaw to an uppercut, which should have torn my head off.

As Willy threw the punch, I got lucky. I'd turned my right knee slightly to keep balance, which also had the effect of moving my head out of the direct line of fire. Willy's uppercut glanced off my left cheek, scuffing the skin, but also throwing Willy off balance.

It had been a knockout blow. All of Willy's impressive power had been behind the punch. If it had landed, I wouldn't have woken up for a week.

In that split second, the fight changed for me. I tucked my head into my shoulders and banged my way off the ropes. Willy was as unprepared for my onslaught as I had been for his. He thought he was going to finish me, but his chance had come, and he'd missed it.

The roar of the crowd suddenly registered in my ears. They had come alive and were screaming their approval of the action. Willy had been circling away to his right the whole fight, slipping my left jabs and not letting me get set to throw anything with my right hand. Abruptly, I switched to hooking my left, stopping his natural movement to the right.

I hooked once, twice, and then threw a straight right. Willy slipped it with his forearm, but I could tell he was unsettled. As a veteran fighter, he'd thought he had me. Instead, I finally had my head in the fight, and Willy could sense the shift.

I was also aware of something new inside me, a cold determination not to give up, back down, or let another fighter have his way with me. The hate and anger that had fueled my fighting for so long hadn't been there against Willy. But this new sensation was even more powerful.

It was as if a switch had been thrown, transforming me from a talented slugger to a seasoned professional. Things I had only sensed before—angles for punches, openings in an opponent's defenses—I could now see clearly. Willy was a great fighter, but I knew I was better.

I remembered who I was: Patrick *Felony* Flynn, the giant killer. And I was not going to lose this fight.

I'd been a fighter all my life, even before being

taken in by St. Vincent's Asylum For Boys. My older brother Mickey and I had survived with our fists on the streets of Chicago. In the orphanage, under the direction of Father Tim, we'd learned to use our fists for the right reasons.

The man who Mickey and I knew as Father Tim *The Battling Priest*, had once been known as Golden Gloves champion Tim *Tornado* Brophy. He used the *sweet science* to teach me and Mickey, and so many other boys, how to be men. He taught us how to accept responsibility, how to believe in ourselves, how to protect those who were weaker, how to never, ever, give anything but our best.

Father Tim's lessons had kept me and Mickey alive on many occasions. Mickey had made a career of the Merchant Marine. He was the champion boxer of his ship, Wide Bertha, as well as every makeshift ring from Shanghai to Havana. As for me, Father Tim's lessons had helped keep the ball of anger I always carried inside me in check until I needed to unleash it.

There were three things in life that had never let me down. They were my brother Mickey, Father Tim, and the power in my fists.

I hadn't seen him, but I knew Archie Moore was in the audience. He was a great champion, and I had to punch my way through Willy to get a shot at him. I wanted my shot. I'd fought for my shot. And Willy wasn't going to keep me from it.

I hit Willy with another straight right. I'd put my shoulder and hips behind it, and the blow was telling. Willy staggered back, covering up, but I didn't give him any time to regroup. I dropped any pretense of defense and raged into an all-out attack.

I threw combination after combination up and down Willy's body. I blasted his arms out of the way and went after his chin and face. This was a new rage to me. It was not the hot rage of anger, but the ice cold clinical rage of the professional boxer.

Willy wasn't going to go down easy. He fought back desperately, but I didn't even feel his punches as they connected. He tried to clinch, but I battered him back. The clock in my head said there were maybe thirty seconds left in the round. I had to put Willy down now.

I threw two rapid left jabs giving Willy the space to circle back to the right, but even as he did, he saw the trap I'd laid. My right was already in motion with all the torque in my body behind it. It was the knockout blow and Willy knew it.

There was no time, but Willy still tried to get out of the way. He pulled his chin in, moving it out of the path of my punch, and lowered his forehead. My punch swept past his chin, landing solid and square on the hard ridge of skull above Willy's eyes.

I felt the force from the blow run from my fist all the way to my shoulder. Willy dropped to the canvas as if all his bones had disappeared. The crowd surged to their feet. The thud of the punch landing had been loud enough to be heard all the way back to the cheap seats.

It completely obliterated the sharp crack of my wrist breaking.

ROUND TWO

THREE MONTHS LATER

The heyday of hobos riding the rails had come and gone in the late '40s. However, even deep into the '50s, the area around the tracks of L.A.'s Union Station harbored many men living the stark hobo existence.

Tombstone was driving our black detective sedan. He pulled it to the curb a block short of the Midnight Mission soup kitchen. The eatery was favored by *traveling men* who didn't have the price of a meal or the cost of a train ticket.

An imposing six-foot-five, Cornel *Tombstone* Jones was L.A.P.D.'s first black detective. He'd been my partner on Chief Parker's *Hat Squad* for the past year, and we'd managed to work well together. Any built-in prejudices I might have developed based on a man's skin color had long ago been driven out of me by Father Tim. Boxing had also helped me lose any racial prejudices thrust at me by society. In the ring, the color of a man's skin made not the slightest difference to the power in his fists or the determination in his *heart.*

Getting out of the sedan, Tombstone opened the back door and retrieved his gray Borsalino. He placed it just so on his head, covering the distinct comma of white falling across his forehead from his otherwise tar black hair. He ran his fingers around the brim of his hat and looked over at me with a smile.

"What are you grinning at?" I asked.

"I liked what I saw in the gym today. You're starting to work your right again."

I retrieved my own black Fedora, set it on my head at an angle, and shrugged. "Still doesn't feel strong."

"You saying Archie Moore has nothing to worry about?"

I was used to Tombstone's style of gentle teasing, but this was a sore subject for me. "I'm saying it still doesn't feel strong."

The break in my wrist from punching Willy Stevenson had been a clean fracture. It healed quickly, but I was tentative about using it. Pops had been on me for several weeks to get back into rhythm with my combinations, but I wasn't ready yet. I didn't know if I ever would be.

"You hear anything from Moore's manager?" Tombstone asked, walking over to join me on the sidewalk.

I shook my head. "I haven't been medically cleared to fight yet. Once it happens, we'll have to see if the bout is still on."

Archie Moore was one of the classiest light-heavyweight champions ever. He would have given me a shot at the title after I kayoed Willy, but my broken wrist had set circumstances on end. There were many other fighters clamoring for their own shot.

Moore was a smart fighter. He didn't need to put his title on the line to a relative newcomer like me, especially as I'd put down the man who had been blocking everyone else's path to the championship. Moore's camp would have to put him up against somebody other than me soon.

I'd unconsciously made a fist with my right hand. I wiggled the wrist back and forth. There was a slight stiffness. Tombstone had been holding the heavy bag for me to punch earlier in the day. He wasn't saying anything, but I suspected he knew I wasn't hitting with real power.

We walked down the sidewalk to the soup kitchen entrance and turned in. There were three dozen men gathered in the large main hall, either sitting on benches or standing in the food line. Conversation and eating stopped when we appeared. Nobody looked at us directly, but they were all aware of our presence.

Father Pedro Cruz, surrendered the soup ladle he was wielding to one of his acolytes and came to meet us. "Detectives, welcome. Thank you for coming." He spoke loudly, his smile as broad as his Hispanic accent. His obvious comfort with us put everyone else at ease, conversation and eating starting up again.

"A full house as usual, Father Cruz," I said, looking around.

The priest shrugged. "They say times are prosperous for many, but not for all." The simple, rough cloth hassock he didn't hide the thinness of his tall frame. The lines of his face told the story of his compassion and empathy.

"Hopefully, this will help," I said, taking an envelope from the pocket of my dark suit.

Father Cruz smiled and took the proffered donation. "Thank you."

It was a small thing on my part. I had no family and my needs were few and simple. My police salary more than covered my costs, and the purse from the Stevenson fight was still untouched in my bank account. Father Cruz was a good man and a good cause.

He waggled the envelope at me. "You do know this is not why I called you?"

"We didn't think it was," I said. "But I know you will put it to good use."

Father Cruz nodded. "Please, come to my office." He turned and led the way.

We walked past the rows of men on simple wooden benches pulled up to scarred wooden tables. They studiously avoided looking at us. Their clothes were shabby, but most had taken some care at cleanliness. These were men clearly down on their luck, but they had vestiges of pride. No doubt some struggled with alcohol and other addictions. Some had been in an out of the state mental hospital up the coast in Camarillo. Some would eventually be taken back there. Some were simply addicted to the nomadic life, riding the rails from town to town, taking odd jobs until the fever to travel on gripped them again.

None of them wanted to interact with the police.

There were no women or children here. There were other sanctuaries for them. Father Cruz's personal mission was with these men. They trusted him, talked to him, confessed to him. Cops or anyone in authority made them nervous, mostly with good cause, but if Father Cruz accepted us, then they trusted his judgment, and we were not considered an immediate threat.

Like the rest of the Midnight Mission, Father Cruz's office was Spartan in its furnishings. There was a simple cross on one wall, two chairs, a small desk, an iron cot with a thin mattress, and a three-drawer chest, all of which were beyond second hand. The rug on the floor was brightly woven and added a touch of warmth, but I knew Father Cruz had done the looming himself.

A man was sitting uncomfortably in one of the straight-backed chairs. His suit was as shabby as those worn by the men in the main hall. The trilby in his hand was battered and frayed. He wore no tie, but his once white shirt was buttoned at the neck. He was a big man, and clearly waiting for us, but he startled as we entered.

"This is Frank Billings," Father Cruz said, starting the introductions. "Frank, these are the two detectives I told you about. You can trust them."

"You didn't say one of them was a nigra." Billings looked ready to bolt from the room.

Tombstone had followed me into the room but had stayed back by the door. He allowed a slow grin to overtake his face, revealing the oversized brilliantly white teeth capped by half-moons of pink gums from whence his nickname came.

"We all gots to be something, *sho-enuf*," Tombstone said. His mother had been a schoolteacher, and he spoke better English than I did. He knew it irritated me when he played the fool, but sometimes it put folks at ease to fulfill their expectations.

"He's big, but he's harmless," I said, more to irk Tombstone than to reassure Billings. "But you, Mr. Billings, you're not so harmless."

Billings stood up. He was a big man, and there were anger and tension in his stance.

"Easy," I said, putting up a placating hand and sitting in the other chair, diffusing the situation. Billings looked slightly confused then sat back down.

"I can see you've been a boxer," I said. "You've got the scar tissue around your eyes and ears to prove it. I can also see from the condition of your hands, many of the fights you've been in haven't involved gloves."

"I don't want to fight no more," Billings said. There was a plea in his voice, which made the blurted statement emotionally poignant.

"Okay," I said. "Who's making you?"

"Crawley."

I looked from Billings to Father Cruz.

"Hiram Crawley," Father Cruz said. "He's the

head Southern Pacific railroad bull."

"King of the Tracks," Billings said. "Any bo gots trouble if he bucks Crawley."

"I know him," Tombstone said from the doorway. "He's free with his fists and his truncheon. Southern Pacific backs him because he keeps a lot of trouble off the tracks."

"That's because *he's* the biggest trouble on the rails," Billings said.

Tombstone nodded. "Heard he was running a shakedown racket, but we haven't paid it any attention since it's small change compared to Mickey Cohen's illegal activities."

"Nobody cares if *bos* got trouble," Billings said. There was a lot of scorn and injured pride in his voice. The hobo culture took far more from a man than it gave; however, it did give the destitute a sense of identity. To identify yourself as a *bo* was to lay claim you were still a man.

"These men will listen," Father Cruz said.

"Why should they be any different?" Billings said with a sneer.

I looked at the man, wondering about the best way to play the situation.

"We don't back down," I said.

Billings looked directly at me for the first time. "Father Cruz says you're the guy chopped down

Solomon King."

I nodded.

"I heard you broke your hand putting down Wil-ly Stevenson," he said.

"My wrist," I said, holding out my right hand and making a fist.

"It going to hold up?"

I shrugged. "Don't know, but maybe we can use Crawley to find out."

ROUND THREE

Billings hit me with a straight right. Maybe I could have swatted it away, but it was a strong shot and we had to make things look good.

Billings was tough for a *bo*. He'd led a hard life on the rails, and it showed in his sinewy muscles and gut determination. But constant undernourishment had taken its toll. Matched up against another *bo* in the same condition, Billings rudimentary boxing skills and determination would probably have seen him come out on top. However, I'd slowed way down so Billings didn't run out of steam before we'd gone two minutes.

We were fighting in an area of the tracks where disused freight cars were stored. A makeshift ring had been squared out using old telephone poles placed flat on the ground. The area was near an established hobo camp. It was visited regularly by traveling men from all over. I was also raided often by Crawley and his pack of semi-tame railroad bulls.

The bulls had caught Billings and me there, which was how we'd ended up pitted against each other in this bare-knuckle contest.

Other *bos* from the camp were gathered around the ring cheering either for Billings or me, depending on which one of us Crawley had pinned their future. Ten of Crawley's uniformed minions stood by. They were tough well-fed men. Their truncheons were drawn, and their Southern Pacific badges hung heavy on their chests as they waited to crack the skull of any *bo* who didn't do as he was told.

Billings and I had railed into the LA depot in an empty cattle car out of Stockton. Tombstone had driven Billings and me up to Stockton despite Billings' assurances we could have ridden the rails north before coming south. However, after spending six hours in an empty, but stinking cattle car, I was glad we hadn't followed Billing's advice and ridden the *blinds* both ways.

Billings was known as a *jungle professor*, a man who had ridden the rails far and wide. He knew every jump-off spot, every free handout location. He knew which bulls were lenient and which ones verged on being killers.

The price of trespassing on the rails was high.

I'd seen the reported statistics. In 1953, Southern Pacific agents had ejected over 600,000 trespassers from the company's trains, often violently. And the Interstate Commerce Commission recorded over 6,000 trespassers killed or injured. There were many others unreported.

Using the information provided by Billings, it hadn't been hard to convince Chief Parker to let our *Hat Squad* unit run a freelance operation against the Southern Pacific Railroad's police. As far as Chief Parker was concerned, there was only one big dog in town—the LAPD.

He didn't care if the Southern Pacific bulls thought they were cops and everyone else thought the hobos were throwaway citizens. Parker hated corruption in any form. He'd created the *Hat Squad*—officially known as the *Gangster Squad*—by bringing together the toughest and straightest cops on the LAPD.

The unit's mandate was to root out all corruption and organized crime in the city. The only rules were to take no bribes, turn no blind eyes, and to use whatever methods were needed to take down anyone who did. For Parker, the ends justified the means. And the Southern Pacific bulls were more than fair game.

The Stockton rail yard had been busy. Despite

the presence of a handful of Southern Pacific bulls, it was known to be hobo friendly. A *bo* didn't get smacked about there simply for riding. If he was caught stealing or vandalizing, then he faced the wrath of the local law. However, if he kept to himself in the local hobo camps, didn't get caught where he shouldn't, and simply hitched a free ride on any of the freights coming and going from all over the country, the law was live and let ride.

The Los Angeles junction was a whole different story.

It was early in the afternoon when Billings and I slipped out of the cattle car as the freight slowed going up the 4th Street hill leading into the enclosed yards. Four other bos were with us. None had shown any interest in me beyond judging if I was a threat to them or not. I was dressed in rough clothing, all supplied by Father Cruz, except for a pair of my own heavy work boots.

I followed Billings and the other bos down a siding and into a makeshift camp. Even though it was still early by hobo standards, I counted twenty-five other traveling men already in the camp. Some were gathered around a rudimentary cooking fire. Others were stretched on the ground, lightly napping in the early afternoon sun. A group of six were engaged in a card game I didn't recognize.

Billings and I had made our way separately to the cooking fire where there was a communal pot of what appeared to be stew. Clearly, the pot was never cleaned. Water and scrounged potatoes and vegetables were continuously thrown into the mix. Several carcasses, bones picked clean were scattered about. I hoped they were rabbits, but they could have just as easily been cats, rats, or small dogs.

I looked into the stew pot. The gray lumps of mystery meat made my stomach turned over. Billings saw the look on my face and laughed. He scooped out a helping with a tin cup he took from inside his ragged suit.

Before he could eat, however, there were shrill whistles and shouts as ten Southern Pacific uniformed bulls charged into the camp. Swearing loudly, they swung their truncheons indiscriminately, kicking with heavy hobnail boots, as they rounded the camp inhabitants into a ragged group. The bulls met little resistance from men used to being despised and abused.

Once the group was tightly packed and contained, Crawley walked into the camp behind his men. I would have recognized him without having seen his picture in the files at LAPD's Central station. He was a big man, easily over six foot four with a barrel chest and a belly that bespoke muscle and power. He had a handlebar mustache slapped across the granite slab of his face beneath a beaked nose and tiny close-set eyes. His uniform was as immaculate as those of his men were sloppy. The black bill of his round cap reflected the overhead sun.

Two of the bulls produced revolvers to threatening to use them if the motley group of bos did not obey. Used to having their own way with the hobos, the bulls were full of bravado. They were corrupt and cruel, like the man they followed.

"You boys will never learn," Crawley said, his voice a gravel filled Scottish burr. He slapped a long hickory baton across his right palm. The baton's leather strap was around his left wrist, making him a southpaw.

One of the bos, a stick-thin man with a pock-marked face, spoke out. "It's just a traveling camp, Mr. Crawley, sir. We'll move on."

Crawley walked up to the man and smiled. I saw the blow coming, but the skinny bo didn't. Crawley's baton only moved six inches, but it was a powerful strike to the man's completely unprotected solar plexus. The bo doubled over and dropped to his knees, retching.

Crawley looked down at the man. "This is my

train yard. You set up camp here; you owe me rent. And you can't ride the Southern Pacific without paying." Crawley turned and walked a few paces. Then he ordered his men, "Split them up and search 'em."

The other bulls cut the gathered bos into two groups. Billings had told me this was likely to happen, and we made sure we were separated. The bulls made the bos empty their pockets onto the ground in front of them. There was an assortment of pocket knives, buttons, and papers. A few coins and an odd crumpled dollar made an appearance here and there.

"I said search 'em!" Crawley roared when his saw the pathetic collection.

This time the uniformed bulls manhandled each *bo*, patting them down and digging hidden cash and coins out of filthy clothing. Everything was tossed onto the ground.

As the two-armed bulls stood guard, others meticulously went through pockets, checked brims of caps, and even detailed shoes and fingered belts.

A hard-working bindlestiff, who'd been following the harvest, was found to be hiding forty dollars. He'd probably planned on taking it home to his family. It was a huge amount by hobo standards, his life savings.

When he pleaded with the bull searching him not to take it, he was thrown to the ground and kicked repeatedly. It was a heartless thing to do.

When a bull with a long face and dirty hair approached me, I stood my ground until he tried to grab me. I deflected his arm and stepped backward. He looked at me angrily and raised his truncheon.

"Don't," I said, in a low voice.

"It'll be me searching you standing or three of us searching you on the ground," he said menacingly. The nameplate on his heavy wool uniform shirt told me his last name was Cotton.

"It'll take more than three," I said calmly. "And they'll be doing it without you."

"What do you mean?"

"You'll be on the ground with a broken jaw." I hadn't flexed my fists yet, but I was ready.

"What's to stop us from shooting you for resisting," he said. His lip curled smugly, as one of the armed bulls turned our way.

In a flash, I stepped forward, slammed the palm of my left hand into his left shoulder, using my right hand to pull his right shoulder forward. My actions spun Cotton around. When he was facing away from me, I looped my right arm around his throat and pulled him back against me. He was off balance and choking as I grabbed my right hand with my left, pulling my right forearm back across his throat.

"Maybe they'll shooting through you to get to me," I said roughly into his ear.

"What's this?" Crawley appeared next to the armed bull, pushing his gun arm down. He gave me a hard look. "You a tough guy?"

"You ain't taking my money," I said. Billings had told me the way things would go if somebody didn't cooperate.

Crawley stared hard at me. I felt he could see right through the borrowed clothing I was wearing and the dirt I'd smeared on my arms and face. It takes a long time to get the ground in grime look of most traveling men. I was worried Crawley would see me as a fraud. Greed and sadism blinds men, however, and Crawley sneered at me.

"If you think I give a damn about ol' Cotton there, you're sadly mistaken. I got no problem killing him and taking you down for his murder. Let him go and you might get out of this alive."

I released Cotton's throat and shoved him forward, making him stumble into the armed bull who fell down trying to catch him.

Some of the other bulls went to move toward me, and I said a quick prayer Tombstone and the rest of my backup were nearby.

Crawley put up a hand and stopped his men from advancing. He walked up to me.

"I like a man with a bit of spirit," he said. "Most of these *bos* are no better than whipped dogs with their tails between their legs. Now, you're going to do exactly as I tell you, or I'll have you busted up so bad you'll never be able to grab another passing freight." He turned and looked over at the other group of *bos*. "You got any contenders over there, Henderson?"

The bull named Henderson pushed Billings out of the group. "Billings here don't want to let us search him either."

Crawley turned back to face me with a shark's smile. "Now, isn't that convenient? What's your name, boy?"

"Flynn," I said without thinking. I felt a line of sweat pop out on my forehead as I cursed myself and hoped Crawley wasn't a fan of the pro fights.

"Billings has been through this before. He's a tough old horse, but you look like you can give him a run."

"I ain't fighting," I said.

"You will fight," Billings said. "Because if you don't, you won't see the sunrise tomorrow."

"You threatening to kill me?" I wanted it plain and in the open.

"I don't threaten, son. I do. These are my tracks, my freight cars, my engines. I can bury you under a ton of coal, and nobody will ever see you again."

Crawley turned and waved Henderson over. Henderson came, pushing Billings ahead of him.

"Here's how this works," Crawley said. "I'm a fair man. Normally, we just take half a *bo's* money in rent and train fare. But I'm in need of a little entertainment, so I'm going to give you boys a little incentive. You fight until one man goes down and stays down. The man left standing gets to keep his money and move on as do the other *bos* in his group. The *bos* in the loser's group lose every cent paying for both groups."

This *entertainment* was nothing new to Crawley and his crew. The bulls herded Billings and me, along with the other *bos*, over to the makeshift ring bordered by the horizontal telephone poles.

I was trying to burn time, wondering when Tombstone and the rest of the squad would put in their appearance.

Prompted by the jeering of the bulls and the *bos* he was representing, Billings came at me had. It was as if he had forgotten we were supposed to be putting on a show to get the goods on Crawley and his crew. Billings threw a series of rudimentary combinations, from which I simply backed away.

He had power in his fist, and he was obviously a tough opponent in the rough and tumble way of untrained fighting men. However, even on a bad day when I'd been with the Navy's Shore Patrol, I could have put him down without breaking a sweat. But this was a different situation. I didn't want to hurt him. But if I wasn't careful, he might hurt me as I tried to maneuver the fight.

I was kicked violently from behind, shoved forward to collide with Billings, both of us falling to the ground. I rolled away quickly and turned to face Crawley. He smirked at me and gave a condescending fake laugh, "Haw, haw." He reached over and grabbed the *bo* nearest to him, a slight man with a club foot. He held him by the neck, forcing him to his knees. Crawley took out a revolver and put it to the man's head. "If you don't quit pussyfooting and start fighting, I'm gonna put this one out of my misery."

I turned to Billings, who had just regained his feet. He swung at me immediately and tagged me on the right cheek. I had just enough warning to turn my head slightly, but the blow still stung. Where the hell was Tombstone?

I batted Billings' next jab away with my right, shooting out my left to hit him in the chest. The point of the chin is the knockout button, but with unprotected fists, it was an easy place to break knuckles.

Billings staggered back, and I moved in on him. Using my big hands as clubbing mittens, I clouted him first over his right ear and then his left. I knew the blows would sting and disorient, but not do any real damage to either him or me.

Crawley fired his gun into the ground next to the man he was forcing to kneel. "I said fight!"

Billings charged me. I waited till the last second then side-stepped like a matador using a *veronica* on a passing bull. As Billings stumbled past, I shoved him hard and sent him crashing into Crawley and the kneeling man.

Crawley stumbled backward, tangling himself up with the three-foot baton he had wedged in his belt. His gun went flying, and I stepped in and hit him with an open-handed roundhouse right with the whip of my hips behind it. He was a big man, but he went down like a headshot elephant.

There were noise and confusion all around me. I realized the *bos* had turned on the Southern Pacific men. Tombstone and the cavalry were also arriving, wielding axe handles as if they were auditioning for spots in the Yankee's line up.

The Hat Squad knew their business. The targets of their axe handles were knees and elbows, not heads. Hit a man in the knee or elbow and he can't fight back. Hit him in the head and he just gets angry.

"About time," I said to Tombstone when he reached me.

"Gate to the yard was locked."

"Your mouth is moving, but the sound coming out of it isn't making sense."

Tombstone shrugged and showed me those big teeth. "All I'm saying is getting here was trickier than it should have been."

"You forgot to bring the bolt cutters, didn't you?"

Tombstone looked down, but he was still grinning. "Yeah. Haskell had to ram the gate four times before it gave way. The front of his sedan looks like it lost an argument with one of these trains."

Detective Roger Haskell could easily be mistaken for a fireplug. Tombstone had brought Haskell and four others from the squad with him. Once they arrived, they were ruthlessly efficient.

The Southern Pacific bulls were rounded up and disarmed. The *bos* had been allowed to scramble back and retrieve their belongings. They were now all sitting on the telephone poles around the makeshift boxing ring.

I personally helped Crawley to his feet. It took a while because he spat at me. As a result, he *ac-*

cidentally fell down—twice—before I got a set of handcuffs on him. Haskell led him away to a paddy wagon.

Several squad cars of uniformed officers arrived as Haskell slammed the paddy wagon doors behind Crawley. He talked with their sergeant and then walked back to us.

"Apparently, the chief wants you two back at the office," he said. "We'll clear up here. Make sure Southern Pacific gets a new crew in."

"Lots of paperwork," I said.

"Story of my life," Haskell said, shrugging his heavy shoulders. "What do you want us to do with the *bos*?"

I looked over to where Billings was sitting. He looked back at me and nodded. "The guy named Billings will be your best witness. Get statements from the rest then deliver them to Father Cruz," I said. "He'll feed 'em and give 'em a bed."

"What do you want the charges to be against the bulls?"

"Book all of 'em for extortion under color of authority. Except for Crawley. Charge him with extortion, assault with a deadly weapon, and filth and ignorance in the presence of a police officer."

As Haskell chuckled, I turned and walked away with Tombstone.

"What do you think the chief wants?"

Tombstone looked over at me and wrinkled his nose. "Probably wants to talk to you about your personal hygiene." He ran a finger around the brim of his Borsalino. "You bringing down the tone of the whole squad."

ROUND FOUR

The Police Administration Building at the intersection of First and Los Angeles streets had finally opened for business two months earlier after being under construction for over ten years. Prior to moving into PAB, the various entities of the police department had been scattered throughout the downtown area. Having an actual headquarters building was helping Chief Parker solidify his power base.

From his office on the seventh floor, he ran the department with an iron fist. His personal mandate as chief was first to take the department back from the corrupt and brutal jack-booted thugs police had become in the '40s, and then take back the city. The first part of his mandate was well in hand, but now he was butting heads with the institutional corruption of the city politicians and gangsters who hid behind them.

For me, the new police headquarters building

was a fresh start. Due to my high felony arrest rate, I'd been promoted from uniformed patrol officer to detective after only three years on the job. The inside track had come because the chief needed my boxing skills in his violent chess game with Mickey Cohen. A detective shield and a spot on the chief's hand-picked Hat Squad had been my reward.

I had a desk in a shiny new squad room down the hall from the chief's office. It might be new, but the squad room wasn't used much. The Hat Squad preferred the bar at Tom Bergin's Tavern on Fairfax. Bergin's had been around since 1936 and had seen generations of cops come and go.

Now, however, I was able to pick up fresh clothes from my locker in the new squad room and was able to clean up with a cat's lick and a promise, as Father Tim used to say, in the restroom down the hall.

Tombstone was waiting for me on a bench outside the chief's office.

"Better?" I asked as I approached.

"Much," Tombstone said, standing. He opened the door to the chief's office's anteroom and ushered me in.

It was late afternoon, but Peggy Parsons, the chief's secretary, was still at her desk. She stood up when we walked in. She was closer to forty than thirty, but she emanated the energy of a much younger woman. She was stylish in a calf-length gray pencil skirt, a flattering red blouse, black seamed stockings, and heels. She took her job as guardian of the gate with deadly seriousness.

"Heard you added another knockout to your record, champ," she said to me, adding a high wattage smile.

"News travels fast," I said. Peggy's husband had been an LA cop killed in the line of duty. She was more than capable of taking care of herself, but everyone on the job looked out for her.

"Go on through," she said, opening the door to the chief's inner sanctum. "He's expecting you."

Chief Parker turned from where he'd been staring out his corner windows overlooking downtown LA. He was a big man, but four years as chief had left a roadmap of stress across his wide features. His black-framed glasses were as no-nonsense as the close-cropped crew cut of his black hair. He wore his uniform like a shield.

Coldly cerebral, he was alternately lauded and reviled for his streamlining of the entire department. He demanded discipline and integrity and had pioneering enforcement of narcotics and civil rights laws. He was intolerant of fools and famously incorruptible. His avoidance of the department's

1950 scandal involving a hundred and fourteen Hollywood pleasure girls had opened the door for his promotion.

Parker nodded at us then moved behind his desk. He picked up a large manila envelope.

"You know anybody in New Orleans, Flynn?"

"No, sir," I said.

"How about Marcus Detroit?" The chief tossed the envelope across the desk to me.

I picked it up and shook out the contents. The photo of a battered dead face looked blindly up at me. I'd seen enough pictures similar to recognize that it had been taken from above a coroner's slab.

The features were unrecognizable due to the battering the face had taken. There was an older scar cutting a finger-wide swath through the left eyebrow. I recognized the scar. I'd given it to Marcus back in the ring at St. Vincent's Asylum For Boys, the orphanage in Chicago where my brother Mickey and I grew up.

I looked at the front of the envelope. The return address was the New Orleans Police Department— the NOPD. I handed the envelope to Tombstone.

I could feel a coldness growing in me. Mickey and I had never been close to Marcus. He'd been a couple of years older, a tough bastard willing to fight anyone over anything. But he was one of Father Tim's boys, and we all stuck together.

"His real name isn't Detroit. It's Marcus de Trod. Detroit was the moniker we hung on him in the orphanage. What happened to him?"

The chief sat down in his chair and leaned his arms on the desk in front of him. "He got himself chopped by a crocodile trying to escape from the Sauvage Federal Penitentiary in a freshwater bayou outside New Orleans."

"Probably a gator not a croc," Tombstone said, slipping the envelope back onto the chief's desk.

Parker gave him a hard look.

"Sorry," Tombstone said, standing up a little straighter.

I pointed at the photo, which had half slipped out of the envelope. "There's only one thing that makes those kinds of facial injuries. Another man's fists."

Parker looked at me. "When was the last time you heard from this guy?"

I shrugged. "Not since he left the orphanage. Ten years ago, or more."

"Then why would he have the words Get Felony Flynn LAPD newly jail tattooed in both armpits?"

"Really? His armpits? Ouch." Tombstone tapered off when Parker looked hard at him again.

I could feel a coldness starting in my heart and moving down to my fists. "Means he had more trouble than he could handle. Knew he wouldn't be around to call me himself."

"Why would he contact you if he was in trouble?"

"You grow up in an orphanage, Chief?" I asked in an even voice.

Parker opened his mouth and then shut it without speaking. Instead, he pushed a smaller envelope across his desk. "Train tickets," Parker said. "New Orleans Superintendent of Police, Colonel Provosty A. Dayries, has only been in the top office a few months, but he's already brought in some ex-FBI hotshot named Banister to clean up his department."

"Is he the one who sent the photos?" I asked.

Parker nodded. "By all accounts, Banister is a hard nose. He once called the Bureau a prostitute who wanted to keep her virginity. He's in charge of the NOPD's internal investigations bureau. He isn't happy about this body turning up chomped on his turf, needle-pointed with an LAPD detective's name. He wants a little help, and we're going to give it to him."

"New Orleans?" Tombstone looked stunned.

"You got a problem with New Orleans?" Chief Parker asked.

"Took my mother nearly ten years to get me out of there," Tombstone said, shaking his big head.

"She isn't going to be too pleased about me going back. This Banister know you're sending him a black detective?"

Parker shook his head. "All he knows is I'm sending two of my best. The man who's named in the tattoo and his partner. I don't care you're black, why should he?"

"Maybe because more than forty percent of the homicides involving black victims in New Orleans are committed by white police officers." Tombstone was getting an odd glint in his eyes. "Maybe because police brutality is accepted, expected, and relied upon to keep us darkies in line, sho-enuf, boss."

Color flushed Chief Parker's face. "They have black officers in their department."

"Since nineteen fifty," Tombstone agreed. "But they're only allowed to patrol colored communities."

"You saying you can't handle this assignment?" Parker asked.

"I'm saying; I put up with more crap in LA than a sewer worker simply because I'm black. You've treated me well, Chief, but I still pay for doing this job. You send me to New Orleans and fists are going to fly."

Parker nodded his head. "I've told you before;

you're no longer black. You're blue. LAPD blue. I expect you to go and do what I tell you. If some eggs get broken along the way, just make sure to clean up the mess."

"Yes, sir," Tombstone said. The expression on his face was a collision of chastisement and pride.

"Why does the LAPD care about a body in New Orleans?" I asked, trying to move the conversation on.

Parker sat back in his chair. "Just because I didn't grow up in an orphanage, Flynn, doesn't mean I don't understand loyalty. Could I stop you going to New Orleans?"

"No."

"Then go and show 'em how we do it here and then get the hell back. We've got more than enough of our own chalk outlines for you to solve."

ROUND FIVE

A National Airlines Douglas DC-6 flew us from Los Angles to Moisant Field on the outskirts of New Orleans in relative comfort. At least for me. Tombstone, white-knuckled his seat arms the entire way. During takeoff and landing, he was whiter than me.

"Taking the train back," he said, as we exited the plane. His voice was little more than a croak, but there was no way I was going to make fun of him. As far as I was concerned, I'd just watched a man conquer his fears.

A metal rolling staircase led us down from the door of the plane into a large, open, hanger-like structure. The humidity was a suffocating wet blanket. Even with my suit jacket off and my tie loosened, my white shirt was instantly soaked with sweat.

Two men, wearing lightweight seersucker suits, straw fedoras, and cop's eyes watched us approach the exit where family members were greeting other passengers. It was clear they were waiting for us. It was also clear they hadn't expected Tombstone.

"Patrick Flynn," I said, extending my right hand. "LAPD. This is my partner, Cornel Jones."

The taller and much thinner of the two men accepted my hand and shook it firmly. "Wallace Ward," he said. "New Orleans PD." The badge parked on his belt next to a holstered .38 was comprised of an interesting star and crescent design. "This is my partner John Quint." He indicated the short, heavyset man next to him. "We work for the department's Bureau of Investigation."

I shook hands with Quint.

"Hell, we are the department's Bureau of Investigation," Quint said.

"Along with Deputy Superintendent Banister," Ward agreed, shaking hands with Tombstone.

When Tombstone extended his hand toward Quint, the NOPD detective turned his back and walked away.

Ward and Quint led us to a standard black, four-door, police sedan. Even driving with all the windows down didn't help much with the heat or the conversation. The ten-mile drive to the city center took twenty sweaty minutes.

Straddling the Mississippi River, New Orleans

was named after a city in Centre, France. It had fought hard to retain its distinct French Creole architecture, as well as its cross-cultural and multilingual heritage. In the early 1800s, thousands of refugees from the Haitian revolution, both whites and free people of color had fled to New Orleans, often bringing African slaves with them.

For years, New Orleans had been a hotbed of racial and urban upheaval, progressing, regressing, and progressing again. All the while, it had retained its unique French and Creole culture. It was sprinkled with Italian and Southern Antebellum flavoring and spiced with superstitions and clashing religions. It was as different from the rest of the United States as the moon from Earth.

When we finally pulled to a stop outside the Criminal Courts Building at Tulane Avenue and South Broad Streets, I was already feeling the spell of the city descending upon me.

Checking locations had been second nature to me ever since I'd first joined the LAPD. The first day on night watch, my training officer suddenly let our patrol car drift into the curb.

When I looked over at him in surprise, he was staring intently at me.

"I've just been shot," he calmly said. "Where are we? When you radio for help, what location are you going to give the units and the ambulance?"

I was mortified. I had no idea where we were. The lesson has stayed with me since.

The Criminal Courts Building was a looming anachronistic structure by LA standards. Its parking lot wound around several stately live oaks draped in Spanish moss. Ward parked the car under one of the trees. We all got out, Ward and Quint still wearing their jackets. Tombstone and I had our jackets draped over an arm, ties at half-mast, and our cuffs rolled up. I had a feeling I was in more danger from the heat than any felon.

There were several pedestrians walking up and down the wide stairs leading to the building's front doors. Like Ward and Quint, none of them appeared to be in a hurry, their pace slow and measured. Maybe it was how they dealt with the heat and humidity but trailing behind the two NOPD detectives I felt as if I was melting into the ground.

When an old woman in black stepped out from behind a pillar at the top of the steps, she moved faster than anything we'd seen since we arrived. She appeared to materialize in front of me after Ward and Quint passed her by. She put a gnarled hand on my chest, one long fingernail slipping between the buttons of my shirt front and making contact directly with my skin.

<Vous êtes le seul,> she said in a harsh whisper in what I knew was French. I didn't speak a word of the language, but I somehow understood every word she said—*You are the one.*

She was a hag, somewhere between fifty and a hundred. She was tall but straw thin, translucently white. Stringy black hair hung in front of startling green, deeply hooded, eyes split by perfectly straight nose. A profusion of beads and bright bangles hung around her neck over the top of the ragged black sheath she wore. Several strands had small leather pouches hanging from them.

She had stopped me instantaneously in my tracks. I might struggle to keep my bulk up to heavyweight standards, but I'm a match for any man. You don't *just* stop me. Her fingernail on my chest was like the tip of a razor. I felt a slight burn and knew she had pierced me.

She whispered again in the same harsh rasp. <Legba told me you would come.> More French. <He will make you strong. Stronger than you are. Stronger than Kalfu.>

A hand reached over the woman's shoulder and spun her around. I felt a tearing as her fingernail left my chest, then a surge, as if a draft had entered the slight wound.

I was frozen in place, watching as Quint, his face

distorted, pushed the old woman back. Her head hit with a crack as he *c-clamped* her throat in the curve his thumb and index finger, pinning her against the pillar from where she had materialized. Her hair flew away from her face, and I saw she wasn't white, but black. Very black. The translucently white image of her face, however, was transfixed in my brain.

I couldn't hear what Quint was saying, but I saw Tombstone's long arm reach out from behind me and his hand pinch the back of Quint's neck. The short, rotund detective's hand released the woman so fast; I knew Tombstone had grabbed a nerve and was squeezing. Hard.

The hag made a quick series of gestures with the fingers of both hands held low. Quint suddenly began gasping for breath, his hands scrabbling at his throat.

"Begone, Mademoiselle Charlotte," Tombstone said, his voice a bass rumble.

The woman turned and fled.

"Leave him be." This came from Ward, his voice a little shaky.

Tombstone turned his head to look at him, malevolence flowing off him, but he released Quint. The detective staggered a couple of steps and leaned against the pillar. Still struggling to catch his breath, he gave a low growl.

"You got something to say to me?" Tombstone asked.

"I said leave him be." Ward was still shaky. But I had to give the man credit. He was covering his partner and wasn't backing down.

"Maybe he should be on a leash," Tombstone said. Then he turned to look at me. "You okay?"

I nodded. I tried to tell my feet to take a step and was finally successful.

"What did she say to you?" Quint gasped. He was beginning to stand up a little straighter.

I smoothed my tie down, covering the tiny spot of blood seeping through my shirt. "No idea," I said. "It all happened too fast. You know her?"

"Crazy Adrieux," Quint said. "She's got two sons, Edmond and Canray, banged up in the Sauvage penitentiary for murder. Creole swamp family. Thinks she can set them free with voodoo. Always hanging 'round, causing a scene. She should be put away."

I knew Tombstone had called the woman something else, but now wasn't the time to ask.

With Quint giving Tombstone the evil eye, we started again for the front doors of the building.

ROUND SIX

The NOPD had commandeered the first two floors of the building. Ward and Quint led us past the front desk, up a set of marble stairs, and on to a series of offices overlooking the front of the building. Ward knocked on a nondescript door, opening it when there was a grunt from inside.

Tombstone and I trailed them into a large space dominated by a huge carved desk. There was clutter everywhere: files, loose papers, newspapers, magazines, bulletins, a safe with the door hanging off the innards of the front lock exposed. I counted four shotguns and six handguns along with box mountains of ammunition. There were two switchblades stuck into different walls, one pinning a sheaf of wanted posters, and the other securing a calendar featuring cheesecake pin-ups. Miss August was particularly pouting and endowed.

The man behind the desk appeared to be as sartorially neat as his office was messy. He came up from behind his desk with purpose. He was a large man with a ruddy complexion, his suit a light tan, his tie a white speckled navy, his shoes buffed to an aubergine gloss. Apparently, he'd ordered his body not to perspire as his shirt was crisp and brightly white.

"Gentlemen," he said, taking in Tombstone with nary a twitch. "Guy Banister, Deputy Assistant Superintendent of Police. Now, isn't that a mouthful." His voice was mellow, Southern accent soft and inviting. His hand when I shook it was as cool and sharp as his shirt.

"Patrick *Felony* Flynn," he said, smiling like a carpetbagger. "What a sweet joy it is to meet the man who took down Solomon King and Willy Stevenson. Archie Moore must be quaking." He had kept hold of my hand with both of his.

I felt a little embarrassed. "I don't think Archie Moore is sweating too much over me."

"How is your hand?"

"My wrist is fine."

"Yes, yes, your wrist." He turned my hand over as if examining it. I pulled it back firmly. I'd expected a suctioning sound when it finally came loose.

Banister turned immediately to Tombstone. "Cornell Jones," he said knowingly. He shook Tombstone's hand in the same two-handed grip.

"Any relation to Muskrat Jones?"

Tombstone looked surprised. "My mother's brother, sir," he said.

I was surprised by the *sir*.

"Knew him well when we were growing up in Monroe," Banister said. "Not more than half a mile separated our log cabins. He still live in Caldwell Parish?"

"I wouldn't know," Tombstone said. He had his hand back, and the missing *sir* hung in the air like Quint's missed handshake at the airport.

Banister took no notice of the slight, but he did take in Quint's disgruntled appearance. "John," he said. "I know Charlotte Adrieux gets under your hide, but that was no way for a Southern gentleman to handle the situation."

Clearly, he had seen us coming from his office windows, which overlooked the front of the building. He turned to look at Tombstone and me. "I'm sure you have your local characters in Los Angeles," he said. He gestured to two chairs in front of his desk. "Please move those papers and sit yourselves down." He looked at Ward. "Wallace, would you take John and get him cleaned up. And have Eunice bring us in some ice tea and lemonade."

Ward and his partner didn't like it, but they obviously knew who was in charge. Once they were gone, the expression on Banister's face changed. He wasn't a carpetbagger any more. He was a tiger.

"You'll have to excuse Detective Quint. He's heavy-handed, but he isn't corrupt, and that's a quality hard to find around here. I understand you two would know a little about a similar situation in your own acre of woods."

"We do," I said from the chair to the right side of Banister's desk.

"Quint is also a bit superstitious," Banister said. "How about you, Detective Jones? Did your mother ever fill you with voodoo tales?"

"I know the tales," Tombstone said. "They're one reason my mother took my brother and me away from its influence."

"Your Uncle Muskrat was once said to be a powerful *houngan*."

Tombstone was silent.

Banister sighed and leaned his considerable weight back in his chair. Appearing to abandon his voodoo track, he said, "I've got three men and a mandate to clean up a department so steeped in corruption, Carlos Marcello might as well be declared Superintendent."

"Marcello is your local mob boss, right?" I asked.

Banister shot me a look. "So, I'm not the only one who does his homework."

I shrugged.

Banister continued. "Anything related to vice in this town gives a taste to Carlos *Little Man* Marcello. I'll get him sooner or later, but right now, I have to deal with him in a much different manner than I would like."

I saw through the doublespeak. "What does he want?"

"Edmond and Canray Adrieux out of Bayou Savauge Federal Penitentiary."

I wasn't sure what this had to do with Marcus de Trod getting chomped by a gator trying to escape. Or why he had my name tattooed in his armpits. But Banister would get there eventually. Men like him always did.

"What's his interest in the Adrieux brothers?" Tombstone asked. "Even if they worked for him, surely they weren't indispensable."

"Marcello's interests have taken some major setbacks since Edmond and Canray were put away for a murder the *Little Man* sanctioned."

"He sees a connection between the two situations?" I asked.

Banister shrugged. "His health has also deteriorated. I understand these physical manifestations have been compared to the trials of *Job*. Charlotte Adrieux appears to have a hold on him."

I raised my eyebrows. "A mobster scared of a hag?"

Banister looked at Tombstone.

I turned my head to also look at him. The whites of his eyes were very pronounced.

"This is New Orleans," he said.

"Exactly," Banister agreed. "This is New Orleans."

ROUND SEVEN

A pinched looking woman in a black skirt and buttoned up white blouse opened the door to Banister's office, breaking the odd silence that had settled over us. She held the door open for a similarly dressed younger woman with similarly pinched features. The younger woman carried a tray with two pitchers and several tall, iced, glasses. She set it on a small table against one wall.

The older woman poured ice tea into a glass and set it in front of Banister.

"Thank you, Eunice," he said. The woman almost cracked a smile. "Gentlemen," Banister asked, looking at Tombstone and me.

I looked at the younger woman standing by the small side table.

"Lemonade," I said.

"Same for me," Tombstone said.

The younger woman poured the drinks and handed one to me. She took the second glass to

Tombstone, standing so far away from him she almost dropped the glass in the exchange. Tombstone smiled at her and said, "Thank you."

"Anything else, Superintendent Banister, sir?" Eunice asked.

"Thank you, no."

The younger woman almost scurried from the room. The older woman followed more sedately. She closed the door behind her, but not before we could hear her start a disciplinary barrage against her younger counterpart.

I took a long drink of the overly sweet, but very cold lemonade. I held the glass on one of the arms of my chair. I felt the cool of the glass seep into my palm in counterpoint to the burning in my chest, which seemed to be spreading. It didn't hurt, but it was there.

I was suddenly tired of the dance. "Superintendent Banister, what's this all about?" I asked, shifting my eyes to the man who sat across the desk from me. "If Carlos Marcello wants the Adrieux brothers out, why doesn't he just buy them out? I'm sure he's no stranger to bribery or violence."

Banister steepled his fingers. It was an unconscious gesture of superiority and always put me on my guard. He appeared to be thinking, but I knew it was a ruse. Banister was a smooth operator. Anyone who had done his background work, finding out exactly who Tombstone and I were and making arrangements to bring us into play, had already done his thinking.

"The Bayou Sauvage is a Federal Penitentiary well outside NOPD jurisdiction and influence," Banister said.

"Shouldn't stop someone like Marcello," Tombstone said.

"No," Banister agreed. "But there is also the problem of Warden Lucas Trask. He grew up in those swamps, and he has turned the Penitentiary into his private kingdom. He is not a man with an interest in those things Marcello is in a position to supply."

"What is he interested in?"

"Fighting. You saw the state of the body of Marcus de Trod. He'd been beaten badly well before the swamp got him. His body isn't the first to turn up on the edges of the Bayou Sauvage. Rumor has it if a prisoner gets out of line, he's forced to fight."

"Fight who?"

Banister spread his hands across his desk. "People are too scared to say."

"Why doesn't the federal government do something about Trask?" I asked.

Banister made a face. "Why should they? The federal government likes having a hole where they can stick the worst of the worst. There are no complaints coming out of Sauvage because nobody comes out. Unless it's like your friend."

"He wasn't my friend," I said.

"Yet, he had your name tattooed in his armpits, and you are here."

I was silent. Anyone who hadn't been raised in an orphanage wouldn't understand.

Banister shrugged his heavy shoulders. "Lucas Trask is a hard man. Prisoners built the prison block by block. There is security, mostly members of Trask's extended swamp family. But even if a prisoner gets out, the swamp will eat them alive."

"What exactly is a swamp family?" I asked.

"There have been people living in and off this swamp for generations," Banister said. "There are many clans, but they all align behind two main families."

"Let me guess," Tombstone said. "The Adrieuxs and the Trasks. Black and white."

Banister nodded. "You grasp the situation."

"Trask does not want to let the Adrieux brothers go."

"They both top seven feet of murderous intent. If they are under Trask's control, they can't be out destroying his moonshine and gunrunning."

It was my turn to speak up. "The warden of a

federal penitentiary runs moonshine and guns?"

Banister nodded again. I had a feeling he thought he was dealing with a couple of turnips off the truck. "Trask turns his nose up at drugs. He doesn't even let them move through the swamp. Which, you can imagine, does not sit well with Carlos Marcello and the mob. Marcello wants Trask shut down for his own reasons, but even with an army of torpedoes he'd never beat Trask's swamp rats."

"Why do you care what happens to Marcello if he doesn't get the Adrieux brothers out of Sauvage?" This came from Tombstone.

"Because Marcello is the devil I know. If I help him with this, he'll give me some of what I want."

"And what is it you want from him?" I asked.

"Corrupt cops. My mandate is to clean up this department, not the town."

Tombstone chuckled, turning over an old axiom. "I hope you know to use a long spoon when you *sup'* with the devil."

"You don't need one if you are the devil," Banister said.

"What do you expect us to do about the Adrieux brothers' situation?" I asked, tired of the posturing.

Banister turned the full force of his gaze upon me.

"I want you to go into the Bayou Savage Federal Penitentiary and break them out."

ROUND EIGHT

We met Danny Romani at the morgue. He was the third detective assigned to the NOPD's small Bureau of Investigation, which made up Banister's anti-corruption team. He was working undercover in Marcello's mob and keeping clear of being seen at the criminal courts building.

He was my height, but at the lower end of the middleweight scale. He was all wiry muscles and long black hair. He looked like a gypsy to my untrained eye, but in New Orleans, he could have been anything.

The morgue was in an ancient building at the end of St. Phillip Street in the French Quarter. Like so many of the other buildings we'd seen in New Orleans, the morgue was ancient. It was also supposed to be haunted. A characteristic I was finding too often in New Orleans.

I was getting a definite case of the heebie-jeebies, especially as the small wound on my chest felt like it was burning hotter. I'd washed it with cold water in a bathroom, but it wouldn't cool down. It didn't exactly hurt, but I constantly knew it was there.

Tombstone and I still hadn't had a chance to talk. After leaving Banister's office, Ward drove us to the morgue and dropped us off. Ward said he didn't need to see the body again. Once he drove away, Danny Romani had approached us and identified himself. My head was still spinning with what Banister had proposed. I figured Tombstone was feeling the same way.

On the slab in front of us was the body of Marcus de Trod, or what remained of it after it had been savaged in the swamp. The signs of a brutal beating were obvious. I knew firsthand what the bruises from gloved punches looked like. The bruises here were magnified, deeper, wider. Whatever fists had caused these were huge, and I'd be willing to bet the gloves around them were weighted with lead.

"Looks to me like I've got the easy job," Danny said. "All I've got to do is let you *kill* me. You've got to go in and face whoever, or whatever, did this." He took in the bruising on Marcus' body with a sweep of his arm.

I hoped I didn't actually have to *kill* Danny, but Banister's very shaky plan called for us to make it look as if I had the following evening in a rigged, *illegal fistic encounter* in a local bawdy house. I'd be arrested for murder and on my way to the big house in short order.

I could tell Tombstone felt the same misgivings as I did. On the surface, all the aspects of Banister's plan tenuously connected. But plans never ran smooth, and when you're inside a hell-hole of a prison, left to your own devises, plans could get you killed.

I looked at the tattoos in Marcus' armpits. Probably done with pencil graphite. Marcus was a heavily haired man, but there was no hair in his armpits, which told me the tattoos were most likely done shortly before he died.

It would have been almost impossible for Marcus to do the tattooing himself, meaning he had to trust somebody else to do the work. Only a few cons had the skills and the steady hand needed to ink tattoos with makeshift instruments, so it might be possible to discover who had done the work. The bigger question was, would the person be an ally?

"How deep are you in Marcello's mob?" I asked Romani.

He looked at me with startlingly blue eyes. "They call it a *krewe* here. I'm on the edges. Nothing more. Hasn't been time."

"You're not from here," Tombstone said.

"Had family here one time. It's why Banister brought me into the NOPD from Chicago. Banister couldn't trust anyone else. Had to be an outsider. Being Italian helped."

"Anyone else know you're NOPD?" I asked.

Danny shook his head, long, straight, black hair, swishing across his features. "Just Banister and Colonel Dayries, the Superintendent."

"How about Ward and Quint?"

"They know I exist. I've never met them."

"How'd you contact Marcello's crew?"

"I got a job on the docks in Port Orleans. Been in the ring like you. Can handle myself as a fighter. Got in a couple of fracases on the docks. Marcello noticed. Got moved up to be one of his torpedoes. Let's me fight on the side in his illegal bouts. Haven't lost yet."

"You sure he doesn't know what side you're on?" Tombstone asked.

Danny shrugged. "I've spent time undercover before. You never know if the bad guys know."

"How do you know I've been in the ring?" I asked. The question was bothering me. I'd never been in a position before where anyone had paid any attention to my fighting. But the destruction of Solomon King, the subsequent pro fights, and especially the bout against Willy Stevenson, had put me in a place where some fight fans recognized me.

"Saw your fight against Willie Stevenson on TV. It was really something. Think you'll get your shot at Moore."

"Have to survive this case first," I said. I felt a heavy sense of foreboding settling upon me. However, as it did the wound on my chest throbbed, and I suddenly felt energized. I turned away and rubbed my chest surreptitiously.

The national sports pages had carried photos from the Stevenson fight. Pop Hawks had pinned them up in the gym until I made him take them down. The bout had also been featured on Gillette's Friday Night Fights. TV was catching on, but they were fairly few and far between. I didn't like the notoriety. Hopefully, they didn't get many newspapers or television reception in the Sauvage.

"Marcello offer you up to take the dive tomorrow?" Tombstone brought things back to point.

"Called me in personally to his house," Danny said. "The man is sick and desperate. He believes the voodoo is on him and he'll die if he doesn't get the Adrieux brothers out of Sauvage."

I shrugged. Before coming to New Orleans, I wouldn't have given you a nickel for voodoo. But we were in New Orleans, and my chest was burning from an insignificant scratch inflicted by a swamp hag. I felt something building inside me. I didn't know exactly what it was, but I felt confident, powerful. I wanted to hit something – or somebody.

Danny left Tombstone and me in the morgue. He slipped out a backdoor, returning to the knife edge of his undercover persona. I knew I would see him again soon enough.

"What do you think?" I asked Tombstone.

"I think I'm starving," Tombstone said. I looked at him and he shook his head slightly.

Then I saw one of the coroner's ghouls loitering by the doorway to the room.

"Let's find food," I said, leading the way out of the building.

The St. Phillip Street sidewalk, which was called a *banquette*, led us down to Decatur. Old oaks lined the street, their branches linked by Spanish moss. Beneath their canopy, brightly colored awnings covered the entries to small shops and the verandas of open-air cafes. The sound of live music, jazz in all its various forms, followed in our wake. It was intoxicating.

Tombstone finally led the way through a somewhat squalid looking doorway into a dark room filled with spicy aromas.

"Why here?" I asked. We had passed several cleaner, glossier looking restaurants.

"Best *etoufee* in town," Tombstone said.

"Is that something edible?" I asked. "And how would you know this place?" There were no other diners occupying the few small tables. Fans turned slowly overhead, making the darkened room marginally cooler than outside.

Tombstone used the entrance of a small black man in a very clean white apron as an excuse not to answer.

The man smiled, showing a row of huge white teeth capped by round pink gums. His size didn't make him a relative, but those teeth sure did.

"Cornel Jones," the man said, hugging Tombstone. "You a man."

When he was released, Tombstone turned to me. "This is Uncle Sirus, my mama's brother. When I knew we were coming, I got mama to give me some contacts to help smooth the way."

"How is Luella?" Sirus asked.

"Healthy, but mad I came back," Tombstone said.

Sirus shook his head and tutted. "That woman never did like it here. She holds a grudge against this entire city. She still have the *eye*?"

Tombstone looked sheepish, an expression I'd never seen him wear before. "If she does, she keeps it hidden."

"Please, sit," Sirus said, seeming to remember his

role as host. He pulled out a chair from one of the half-dozen small tables. "I bring you food."

"For three," Tombstone said, as Sirus scurried away.

"Three?" I asked.

"You didn't see her?"

"Who?"

There was a shadow in the doorway, and then Charlotte Adrieux slid into the chair Tombstone was holding out.

ROUND NINE

She smiled at me, and I had to blink to keep her in focus. "Sit," she said, her voice that of a much younger woman, gently commanding. "We will eat."

I sat. I had no idea why I did whatever this woman asked, yet I didn't feel threatened by her. All I knew was she was now speaking English.

Sirus reappeared with bowls of what Tombstone had called *etoufee*. It smelled marvelous. Tombstone had already dipped his spoon in and was enjoying his first mouthful.

He saw me hesitating. "It's a thick roux," he said. "Rice, tender chicken, and vegetables. Spicy stew."

I dug in. It was amazingly good, but I needed lots of drinking water to go with it. Sweat popped out on my forehead. Spicy wasn't even close.

Nobody talked until our bowls were empty and Sirus had cleared them away. He left us with glasses filled with a thickened liquid he called *acassan*.

"Acassan?" I asked Tombstone, no doubt butchering the pronunciation.

"Boiled cornmeal sweetened with highly refined cane juice," he said. "It will take the sting out of the spices."

Charlotte Adrieux picked up her glass with a smile. *<How sweet of you to remember,>* she said, this time reverting to French.

"What is going on?" I asked Tombstone. "She's speaking French. How come I can understand her? Why did you call her Mademoiselle Charlotte at the courthouse?"

Tombstone looked straight at me. "Voodoo," he said, his voice flat, a slight inflection of a dare.

The hag reached out and placed her hand on my chest over the small cut she had inflicted earlier. My organs felt as if they were swelling, but I couldn't pull away from her. *<Be still, child,>* she said, her voice a soothing lilt. *<You have been chosen. You are getting stronger. Legba is in you. Do not fear him.>*

"Tombstone?" I croaked out.

"Charlotte Adrieux is my mother's cousin. She has always been a channel for Mademoiselle Charlotte—a loa, a white European voodoo spirit."

Charlotte chuckled, her hand still on my chest. *<I saw Cornel born. Such a sweet child. He knows I protect him. He don't forget what I like to eat and drink. He*

treats me like a lady.>

She took her hand from my chest, but the feeling of power continued to swell inside me. I felt feverish. My eyes blurred, and Charlotte's features became younger, her skin tone lightening perceptibly. A second passed and the hag was back.

"What dat man tell you 'bout my sons?"

I assumed she was talking about Banister. "He said they were put in Sauvage for murder."

"My sons no murder. Trasks did it." She spat on the floor. "Trasks lie. They say my boys did it; then they lock them away. Lucas Trask follows Kalfu...is Kalfu." Charlotte Adrieux stopped speaking, then looked at me like what she said made sense.

I turned to Tombstone. Sweat trickled down my cheeks; my whole body felt like a furnace. Tombstone's face showed concern as well as something I'd never seen in him before—fear.

"Legba and Kalfu are twined." Tombstone said. "Legba controls the positive spirits of the day. Kalfu controls the malevolent spirits of the night. Kalfu is the grand master of charms and black magic sorceries. He has the ability to change people into animals and control their minds. Legba is the guardian of the forces of the universe, the god of destiny."

"You believe all this?" I asked, trembling.

"I don't disbelieve," Tombstone said.

And then I felt flames stealing my breath and I fell into the sun.

***

I became fully alert the moment I awoke. I snatched away the cool cloth covering my eyes and sat up. I swung my legs over the side of the low bed I had been lying on.

"Easy," Tombstone said. One of his large hands steadied my shoulder.

"Thirsty," I said.

Tombstone lifted a pitcher from the cabinet next to the bed. He went to pour the contents into a glass, but I took the pitcher from him and drank directly from it.

After a dozen swallows, I came up for breath.

"Where are we?"

"Boarding house. It belongs to another of my mother's cousins."

"Big family."

"You have no idea. How do you feel?"

I took a second and did a mental and physical check. I shook my head, bemused. "I feel terrific," I said. "What time is it?"

"You've been gone all night and most of the morning. It's coming up on noon."

"The fight?"

Tombstone smiled. "Plenty of time."

"What happened last night?"

"You were with Legba."

"Come on. Not more voodoo."

Tombstone sighed. "There are things that can't be explained. We are caught in the middle of them. My mother warned me this would happen."

"Smart woman," I said.

Tombstone gave one of his throaty chuckles. "Don't I know it. Voodoo is why my mother left New Orleans. She is a strict Catholic and hated the way her religion had become syncretized with voodoo in Louisiana and elsewhere."

"So, she didn't believe in voodoo?"

"She believed it took my father. Our family was rife with it. My father was an Adrieux."

"But your last name is Jones."

"My mother left the Adrieux name behind when she left the swamp."

I thought for a second then said, not unkindly, "You're saying your mother can take the boy out of the swamp, but she can't take the swamp out of the boy?"

"I'm saying; something stinks about this whole scheme of Banister's."

"He says he has the power of the FBI waiting to descend on the Sauvage Penitentiary for violations of federal law. He wants me to go in to protect the Adrieux brothers because he thinks Lucas Trask will kill them rather than see them released."

Tombstone nodded. "And how does that sound in the light of day without his carpetbagger's oily sales pitch?"

He was right. But after a beat I said, "I still have to go in."

"Why?"

"You know why."

"Marcus de Trod," Tombstone acknowledged.

I shook my head. "Yes, but..."

"But what?"

I could see in his eyes Tombstone knew the answer. I felt the life heat in my body. I was a fighter. A strong fighter. I'd fought in the worst hell holes the world had to offer. I had never backed down from a fight. I was Patrick *Felony* Flynn, the giant killer. But now, inside, I was also something more.

"Legba," I said. "Destiny."

ROUND TEN

The Chateau Lobrano d'Arce was a four-story frame mansion. It rose up alongside similar residences on North Basin Street but was distinguished by an onion-domed cupola. It was nearing midnight. The brothel housed inside the residence was heaving with customers, sight-seers, button men, and what Father Tim back at the orphanage called *bawdy women*.

Adele LeDoux, the owner of the brothel, was a tightly-corseted, light-skinned black woman. Her sausage-like arms sprouted from beneath the cap sleeves of her red velvet dress, matching the equally jiggling display of flesh making up her cleavage.

Tombstone had told me prostitution had been legal at one time in the Storyville area of downtown New Orleans. It had been controlled, licensed, and very profitable until the federal government enforced a stop. What the federal government couldn't stop were corrupt politicians. Prostitution continued to flourish in New Orleans with politicians, police, and prosecutors all paid to turn a blind eye. There were occasional police raids designed to garner headlines, but these came with advance warnings—much like tonight's planned fiasco.

I wasn't paying much attention to the surroundings. I was busy in the makeshift ring erected in the main parlor.

We were in the third round. Danny Romani was obviously more of a local favorite than he'd let on. He was a better fighter than I'd expected. I outweighed him and had a lot more experience, but he was quick and could take a punch. I knew it was going to hurt his pride to take this dive. It was clear, however, he planned to make a good showing for himself before hitting the canvas.

The audience surrounding the ring had come to see a real fight. I was puzzled at first, but then remembered the animosity between the Italians and Irish in New Orleans ran deep.

The most violent of their encounters took place sixty years earlier when the Irish chief of police, David C. Hennessy, was assassinated. A sensational trial followed, resulting in *not guilty* verdicts for the nineteen Italian men on trial. The fury of an enormous Irish mob was ignited. They rioted in the streets, forcing open the prison doors and lynching eleven of the men who had been indicted but cleared of Hennessy's murder.

The Irish called the lynching *justice*. The Italians called it a *vendetta*.

Judging by the animosity of the two main ethnicities of the crowd tonight, the incident might have occurred yesterday. While I was keeping on my toes handling Danny, brothel bouncers were having a hard time keeping the Italian and Irish spectators separated.

The huge parlor covered the first floor of the structure. A bar ran the length of one wall, and there was a small kitchen annex off to one side. On a jerry-rigged platform above the bar, a six-piece band was cranking out Dixieland like their lives depended upon keeping the music going.

Danny tried to barrage my midsection, but I pulled him into a clinch. We waltzed around until the referee, a short, round, muscle of a man with a fussy mustache and soft pink hands, forced us apart.

"Fight," he said. Forced around the stub of a cold cigar clenched in his teeth, the word came out like an explicative.

Banister said the fight was easy to arrange. Boxing matches were a regular Thursday night feature of the Chateau Lobrano d'Arce. Both scheduled opponents for tonight's scheduled bout were curiously sick or injured and unable to toe the line. Danny, a known and liked commodity who had fought in these bouts before, was an acceptable replacement. On the other hand, under the name *Irish Mike Brophy*, I was the villain. An Irish outsider on Italian turf. I hoped Banister knew what he was doing and could control the mob when Danny went down. Otherwise, I might not survive to go to prison.

Danny took a swipe at me as we parted, but I pushed the punch aside and delivered a rabbit punch to his kidneys. He grimaced and danced away. I'd let him know who the pro was here. He was beginning to catch on. This was good. If he realized I could put him down any time I wanted, it would take the edge off his ego and make his eventual role easier to take.

Boxing is not about simply delivering punishment. It is equally about avoiding or absorbing punishment. An untrained street fighter stands little chance against a conditioned boxer. From the backstreets of Chicago and LA to every military dive bar in far off places around the world, I'd learned to avoid and absorb punishment. I was not afraid of being hit. I'd often allow myself to get tagged in order to create an opening to deliver double the punishment to my opponent.

However, tonight, I was amazed at the strength in my legs, the power in my arms, and the speed of my reactions when Danny came at me. I shouldn't have been this sharp. I'd been working out in the gym and running. But all the sparring I'd done since my wrist healed had been ashamedly half-hearted.

But the vitalizing burning in my chest was a constant presence. Since the start of the fight, I'd also been feeling it in my right wrist. My whole right fist inside the cheap boxing glove was tingling with fiery pins-and-needles. Every time I hit Danny with it, it felt stronger. It felt like it couldn't wait to hit again. I'd never been this clearheaded.

A bell clanged, sending Danny and me to our respective corners. Tombstone was waiting with my stool, water, and a towel.

He was garnering an abundance of fierce looks. There were a few other negro men in the crowd. There were others amongst the musicians and kitchen workers. But all of them were subdued and watchful. While the house was run by a black madam and there were several Creole working girls, Tombstone had told me negro men were expected to satiate their lust elsewhere in negro only establishments.

"How are you holding up?" Tombstone asked. "You're looking sharp."

"Feel sharp," I said.

"Legba in you," he said.

"If so, I hope he never leaves."

Tombstone toweled me down. I spat water I'd rinsed my mouth with into a bucket.

"This round, you put him down," Tombstone said. "You know I don't like this plan."

I nodded. "I know, but it's going to happen. Can't stop it now."

"Yes, we can."

I shook my head. "Get yourself clear but be there when I need you. We both know we can't rely on Banister. This whole thing is a farce, but Marcus is still dead, and I will get to those responsible."

Tombstone shrugged. He knew me too well. "As soon as Danny goes down, I am going into the swamp with Charlotte," he said. "I don't want to get tied if Banister plans to neutralize me."

I smiled at Tombstone. "Neutralize you? He'd have a better chance of petting an enraged gator. Don't get lost out there in voodoo land."

The clang of the bell overrode Tombstone's laugh.

ROUND ELEVEN

I came out of my corner raging. I felt strong and powerful. Archie Moore wouldn't stand a chance against me tonight. Danny Romani, a kid fighting above his weight with delusions of grandeur, wasn't even a threat.

As soon as I was close enough, I let loose a barrage of punches to Danny's midsection. He tried to counter, to push me away, but he couldn't move me. Part of me was aware I had to make the fight and the supposed killing punch look good. But another part of me, a part I was having trouble controlling, wanted to explode murderously and really kill my opponent.

Danny was all over the place against the ropes completely defenseless. Somehow, I reined in my aggression and eased off. I let Danny clinch, waltzing with him until he got his feet and his breath back.

"Sweet mother," he gasped in my ear. "I never fought nobody like you."

And I'd never fought like this before. I was a strategist, not a brawler. I could go a little berserk when needed, but my usual style was to pick my punches, find my opponents weaknesses, and exploit them. If I did, then the knockout would eventually come. But tonight, I was on a rampage.

The crowd was screaming approval, cheering the blood from the split I caused to Danny's right eyebrow. I'd burst it open like an overripe tomato, and gore was flowing down his face.

Then I saw the look in Danny's clear eye. He was scared. I had stripped him of his confidence, broken his arrogance. He believed I might kill him. I had to do something quick before he lost his nerve.

I feinted with my left. Danny's defense was in such confusion he immediately bought into it. He moved to block it, which gave me an open straight line between the point of his jaw and my right fist.

Without hesitation, I shot a pile driver jab straight to the point of Danny's jaw. He was so unprotected; the punch could have torn his head from his shoulders. I'd thrown the jab not just from my shoulder, but from my hips and my braced right leg. At the last split-second, I pulled it before contact, stopping the turn of my hips short of a full swivel. Still, I felt the bone of Danny's chin sink deep into my glove before he launched backward.

His feet came off the floor. He flew like a rag doll to collapse on the canvas. He was down. Out. I immediately wondered if I'd pulled the punch enough.

There was a moment of stunned silence from the crowd before they broke out in an uncontrolled roar. As they did, there came the sound of whistles and the blaring of police voices. There were uniformed officers everywhere, breaking up the crowd and cracking heads when they didn't get cooperation.

I took a quick glance around, but Tombstone was already gone.

Wade and Quint, stepped through the ring's sagging ropes with several uniformed officers. One of the uniforms grabbed the referee and handcuffed him. In a booming voice, Quint declared the fight crowd an unlawful assembly and the fight an *illegal pugilistic exhibition*. It was all mumbo-jumbo for the sake of appearances.

Wade was standing over Danny's prostrate form as the house doctor knelt next to the young fighter. The doctor checked for a pulse in Danny's wrist, then along the carotid artery in the neck.

"This boy is dead," The doctor said loudly, turning toward me. "You killed him."

I felt a little touch of panic. I knew the doctor and both Quint and Wade were in on the deception, but

I also knew I'd hit Danny hard. Maybe too hard. I swallowed, hoping I hadn't really killed him.

The crowd renewed their roaring, and there was debris being thrown everywhere. Quint made a clumsy grab for me, but I pushed him aside. He growled and came back at me, swinging a cosh. I couldn't help myself. He was so slow, and the adrenaline was still coursing through my body. My left fist shot out and hit Quint in the throat. He gagged and went down.

Wade raced at me from across the ring as three uniformed officers swarmed me. I scuffled for a few moments, then went down to the canvas under the sheer weight of bodies. The officers were clearly not in on the deception. They poured blows and kicks down upon me as I curled into a fetal position, tucking in my chin into my chest, bringing my forearms up to protect my face, and wrapping my gloves around my head.

Eventually, Wade pulled the officers away and dropped a knee down on my back. "Don't move," he hissed. "Or you won't get out of here alive."

He pulled roughly on my arms and got my hands cuffed in front of me. "Irish Mike Brophy," he said in a clear, ringing voice. "I'm arresting you for the murder of Danny Romani during the course of an *illegal pugilistic exhibition.*"

ROUND TWELVE

The prison truck was a clapped-out Ford with bald tires and a ruined suspension. There were two of us sitting opposite each other in shackles on benches in the back. The sides of the canvas covering had been rolled up over metal ribs and tied to the canvas roof. The open sides did nothing to abate the stifling heat, serving only to allow the mosquitoes free range as we moved slowly down the badly rutted road.

I was wearing rough, gray, prison clothing. My hands were manacled in front of me, my feet shackled to a chain running down the center of the truck bed. I was sweating profusely and being eaten alive by insects.

The window in the back of the cab had been knocked out, making it easier for the passenger guard to put his shotgun on us, *"Iffin* you get uppity."* He was scarecrow thin with bad teeth and a wandering eye. The shotgun he caressed might be more dangerous to himself than to any prisoner.

The driver guard was clearly the alpha of the pair. His belly lopped over his belt, but he carried himself light on his feet in the way of some fat men. Both wore faded tan uniforms with Federal Corrections' shoulder patches, generic badges, and thick black gun belts heavy with firearms, truncheons, and big keys.

Both of their name tags read *Trask*. From listening to them, I knew the driver was Calvin, and the scarecrow was Deke.

The eight-foot wide road was the only way to and from the penitentiary. The edges were bordered by prisoner broken rocks, which barely held back the brackish water of the Bayou Sauvage swamp.

East of New Orleans, captured between Lake Pontchartrain to the north and Lake Borgne to the south, the 23,000-acre Bayou Sauvage was a hell hole of wiregrass, hardwood and gum trees. It was teaming with birds, and stinking water filled with snakes and alligators. Spanish moss was everywhere, and the smell of rotting vegetation was as oppressive as the humidity.

The prisoners from Sauvage Penitentiary were made to build and maintain the swamp's hurricane levees, which protect New Orleans from flooding. If their slipshod care of the road were any indication, the city wouldn't be safe from a rainstorm let alone a hurricane.

I was seriously rethinking my loyalty to Marcus de Trod.

It was likely Marcus did whatever it was to get him sent to the Sauvage. However, my presence in the back of the truck showed how easy justice could be perverted...or *accelerated*, as the judge who sentenced me for *killing* Romani had phrased it.

I knew I hadn't killed Romani. As his body had been hurried out of the ring, away from the press of photographers, I'd seen his eyes open and contact mine. He'd been out for the count, but not for the long count where St. Peter was the referee.

In the ring, after Ward had fastened cuffs to my wrists, I'd been as unceremoniously hustled away as Romani's limp body had been.

Things were supposed to move slowly in the heavy southern heat. But the New Orleans justice system seemed as eager to sentence me as the tabloids were to crucify me. Banister managed to release only bad pictures of me to the newspapers, hoping I wouldn't be recognized. There was some tampering with the stories the reporters wrote, as they were as easily misdirected by a dollar as everybody else.

I was tried and convicted in less than a week.

New Orleans claimed not to have a facility to keep a dangerous killer like me locked up. Their petition to transfer me to the Sauvage took only another politically expedited week.

And all the time, the strange heat in my chest never left.

I had come to feel it as a comfortable warmth. It kept everything at a distance—pain, worry, fear. It had become a part of me. I could no longer remember what it felt to be without it. I no longer wanted it to go away.

"You that *Irish* Mike Brophy feller who *kilt* that boxer?" This question came from the man sitting across from me. I'd heard the transport guards call him Martin Crebbs. He was a short, wiry, scrapper. His pale skin was reddened and freckled, his accent fresh from Dublin.

I shrugged. "They called it murder because the fight was illegal, but nobody forced him to face me."

Crebbs nodded, thinking over my statement.

"You've been in the ring," I said. It was obvious from the scarring around his eyes and the cauliflower shape of his right ear.

"Just another pug," he said. "Fought flyweight. Lost more fights to bleeding than knockdowns."

I could see the ridges of his eyebrows, the target for any opponent. Split those open, and if a cut man couldn't staunch the blood between rounds, the referee would call a forfeit.

"How'd you end up here?" I asked. The truck lurched through a series of potholes. The wooden bench I was on wasn't built for comfort or balance, especially when shackled.

"Came over on a beer barge. Jumped ship to see the sights."

I'd heard of the supply ships called beer barges. They delivered Irish beer to the thirsty throats of Irish ex-pats, who drank enough to make the trips profitable.

I raised my manacled hands. "And what happened?"

"Ah, worst luck. I *kilt* a whore who stole my wallet." He said it as if it was her fault. "I had my knife on her, but she wouldn't give it back. She tried to get away and ran into the point of the blade, the silly cow. Should have only been a nick, but it got an artery. Like I said, worst luck."

I'd heard variations of his statements from almost every thug I'd ever arrested. It was never their fault. They were all innocent. It was simply bad luck, or somebody made them do it.

I felt my stomach do a flip-flop, aware again of the dangers around me. In the Navy, and with the LAPD, I'd put more than my share of men in the brig and in the prisons. I never planned on ending up on their side of the bars. If any of the cons in the Sauvage found out I was a cop, I wouldn't last an hour.

I had to stop thinking and acting like a cop. I had to think like Crebbs and all the others like him. The irony was, I was *innocent*, but nobody was going to believe me.

I had a week to work out something for the Adrieux brothers and discover what happened to de Trod. The second the week was over, Bannister promised to thunder down on Bayou Sauvage Penitentiary with all the power he could muster from his FBI days. His plan was to dismantle the Trasks' stranglehold on the prison's administration and burn up the headlines with his reforming hardline. This conveniently overlooked his mandate to reform the NOPD itself. Instead, he was in bed with the head of the local mob conspiring to take down a common enemy.

The politics were not my concern. Chief Parker had given me and Tombstone a job to do—clean up the murder of Marcus de Trod, whatever it took. It was a job I'd do anyway because Marcus was St. Vincent family. Father Tim never let us forget we were family. We could have our squabbles, and we did. Sometimes, we verged on hating each other.

But, if you had been in the ring with someone at St. Vincent's, you were their brother, and you didn't let them down. Ever.

Tombstone would also be here. He and I were a different kind of family. The family of the badge. There were tough street gangs in LA. Mob boss Mickey Cohen was in LA with his crew of bent-nose thugs. But those of us who were blue through and through were part of the biggest, toughest, meanest gang in town. We backed down for no-body. If we ever did, we wouldn't survive.

I'd long ago learned Tombstone had his own net-work of contacts. Sheer talent went a long way, but I knew it took more than being a great detective for Tombstone to become the first Negro detective on the LAPD. While I'd been in the Navy, Tombstone had been in the Army saving the lives of two future congressmen, a future senator, and the son of a four-star general. Tombstone had a political pull at a level rare for a man of color.

Banister was playing fast and loose with the truth, with my freedom, and ultimately my life. He would abandon me to the wolves as soon as it was politically expedient, but Tombstone, and those in power who owed him, wouldn't let him.

Tombstone and I were bound tighter than blood. Tighter than race. Wherever he was, Tombstone would be coming for me. And he would be bringing the apocalypse with him.

I felt the truck begin to slow. I leaned backward to see around the cab. Ahead, on one side of the road, were twelve ragged men in prison grays. Their feet were shackled. Half of them were using heavy sledgehammers to smash a line of boulders into smaller rocks. Two other men were taking the smaller rocks, walking down a mud levee extending out from the road, and placing them on top of other rocks along the base.

A heavy-duty prison pickup truck was parked on the side of the road behind a battered, ex-military, Jeep. The remaining four prisoners were working together to roll heavy boulders out of the truck bed, dropping them on the road for the other prisoners to smash.

There were two guards in tan uniforms wearing trooper hats and sunglasses. They were leaning against the truck. Both held shotguns. Floating on the swamp were two boats, each manned by a rifle-toting guard.

The first boat was a narrow, oblong, skiff. It was twenty feet in length with a blunt bow and stern, a flat bottom, and slightly flared sides. There was a two-cylinder engine attached to it.

The other boat was completely different. An

open, flat bottomed, rectangular boat, it was a floating platform with a propeller engine mounted on the back. The driver sat in an elevated position in front of a cage to protect him from leaning back into the large propeller blades. The locals called it an airboat.

The truck Crebbs and I were in came to a stop when the Jeep pulled out and blocked our progress. A very tall, powerfully built man stepped out of the Jeep. His tan uniform shirt stretched across an unnaturally wide chest. Two Alsatian dogs followed at his heels.

He wore tan cavalry pants tucked into knee-high leather boots, which gleamed with polish. The short sleeves of his shirt were tight around massive biceps. His black hair was long for a man in uniform. It was combed straight back and fell below his shoulders. More interesting were the layers of beads he wore around his neck, swooping down across his shirt. There were three leather thongs among the beads, each supporting a small leather pouch.

His face was a carved monolith, all jaw and forehead. He wore no hat or sunglasses. His eyes were black dead pools on either side of a strong nose, which was distinguished by a knuckle-sized bump near the top.

The heat in my chest flared, and I knew instinctively who this was—Warden Lucas Trask. The devil made flesh.

He walked slowly down the side of the truck I was in. He was carrying a Winchester rifle casually in one hand. The two large dogs padded silently after him. All rock breaking and work on the levee had stopped. None of the guards spoke. Trask himself was silent as he stopped, first looking at Crebbs and then at me.

He stared at me for a long time. I stared back. The burning in my chest made me feel I could break the shackles restraining me and attack. I forced myself to sit stoically, waiting. Trask broke eye contact and produced an engaging smile, his eyes sparkling in the sun. Then he snapped his fingers and pointed at Crebbs.

Deke immediately got out of the passenger side of the truck, almost tripping over himself in his haste. He climbed into the truck bed and used a large key to unlock Crebbs' foot shackles. Leaving Crebbs hands manacled, Deke roughly pulled him to his feet and forced him to jump down from the back of the truck. Crebbs stepped sideways, watching Trask and his dogs.

Trask levered the action on the Winchester, putting a shell in the chamber. One of the dogs growled.

"What's this about?" Crebbs asked. He could not hide the quaver in his Irish lilt.

Trask waggled the fingers of his right hand, and the growling dog moved forward. When it was three feet from Crebbs, it bared its teeth and snapped several rapid barks.

Crebbs automatically backed up.

Trask waggled the fingers of his left hand. I noticed only three were complete. The pinky and ring finger were stubs. The second dog moved forward. It was silent, but its lips were pulled back to reveal sharp incisors.

Crebbs backed up again. "Sweet Mary, there's no need for this now. Whatever you want, I'll do it."

"Can you bring my whore back to life?" Lucas Trask asked in the same low register as the growls of his dogs. He cocked the trigger on the Winchester.

"I didn't kill her." Crebbs' manacled hands were out in front of him, pleading. The dogs herded him back to the edge of the road. "It was an accident. She stole my wallet."

"Not the way I hear it," Trask said. His voice was dead calm. He whistled a shrill note, and the dogs began to force Crebbs down the road a few paces, then off the road until he was ankle deep in swamp water.

"I hear you took what you wanted from Sylvie without paying. Then you struck her and took her evening's earnings. My earnings."

"No!"

The dogs were at the edge of the water. Crebbs was now crotch deep in the swamp.

"I didn't kill her. She came at me. It was an accident." Crebbs was crying. His fear of the dogs and the snot from his nose making his Irish accented words indecipherable.

Trask was silent for a moment. His eyes were watching the swamp as if waiting for something. Then he spoke. "An accident? I didn't realize."

"Thanks be to the saints." Crebbs' relief was plain.

There was a violent movement in the water behind him, and the jaws of a huge alligator snapped around Crebbs' waist. The Irishman didn't even have time to scream before the gator rolled him under with a thrashing of its tail. One second Crebbs was there. Then there was nothing but a swirl of water. An arm shot up from the swamp ten yards further out, only to disappear again immediately.

The dogs had moved back to sit at Trask's feet. He turned toward me. He was fingering one of the leather pouches hanging from around his neck.

"Funny thing accidents," he said. Then he began to laugh in a high-pitched peal. He turned a complete circle, waving his arms up and down, encouraging everyone to laugh with him. They all did, guards and prisoners alike.

Facing me again, he stopped laughing as if he'd turned off his funny tap.

His black eyes bore into me. "Welcome to the Sauvage."

ROUND THIRTEEN

The Bayou Sauvage Penitentiary was an ugly, functional, structure. The walls enclosing the compound were made from weathered gray brick topped by razor wire. Parts of the walls were in crumbling disrepair. There was a sentry tower in each corner.

I figured we were three miles deep into the swamp. The lone road led directly to two huge wooden doors. They swung inward to admit first Trask and his dogs in his Jeep, then the truck in which I was shackled. Behind us came the truck carrying the chain gang.

Inside the walls, things didn't get any prettier. The compound's blood colored earth had been reclaimed from the swamp. There were two long cement block buildings, running parallel. One building was two stories, clearly the cellblock for the two-hundred prisoners forgotten in the Sauvage—murderers, rapists, and violent bank robbers to a man.

PAUL BISHOP

The building opposite had to be the guard's quarters and the administration offices. I could also see what must be the prison laundry and cookhouse. What was surprising was the back wall of the prison had a large open break in the middle. Beyond the break in the wall was a dock made from wooden planks lashed to vertical wooden posts. There were three airboats tied up to the dock alongside two flatboats. There was a silo on either side of the break, each with its own armed guard at the top.

To one side of the dock, I could see the Sauvage's version of a prison work program. It was a huge distillery for making the corn whiskey known as *white lightning*. Banister had said Trask used the prisoners to run the distillery, keeping a daily line of trucks, flat-bottomed skiffs, and airboats filled with the illegal hooch to be delivered. It was floated out across the swamp or driven away down the one road in and out of the prison.

There was another more noticeable structure, which grabbed my attention. In the center of the open courtyard was a huge square cage formed with three-inch diameter iron bars. They were sunk into the ground and extended ten feet high. More bars were latticed across the top and used to make doors into the cage on opposite sides. The scuffed, hard packed dirt enclosing ground was close to twenty square feet.

Father Tim had once taken a group of St. Vincent's boys to see the Ringling Brothers' three-ring circus when it passed through Chicago. One of the circus' rings had been filled with the lion tamer's cage. The ugly, ominous, structure in the middle of the Sauvage's courtyard reminded me of a nightmare version. A vision made more real by the rows of closely bunched benches surrounding it. There were two narrow pathways through the benches ending at the cage doors on either side.

My chest began to throb when I saw the iron bar cage. The heat inside me was rising. I knew I'd soon be inside those bars fighting for my life.

I should have felt the fear it was built to encourage. But I didn't.

Instead, I felt a raging lion inside me, furious to get out and destroy whatever man with a puny whip and chair who dared get in the cage with me.

My observations were abruptly ended when Deke reached in and unlocked my foot shackles from a hook in the truck bed. I was left with four feet of chain between my feet connecting to the iron cuffs around my ankles. Walking was more of a careful shuffle.

Without talking, Deke led me to the long building on the left side of the prison. In the interior, rows of cells ran down either side of a long wide walkway. A second row of cells ran along the tops of the ones on the ground floor. The walkway was running in front of the second story of cells extended over the cells below, making them cooler, but darker.

As Deke shuffled me along the walkway, men in the cells moved to see the new addition to the population. It was eerily quiet. I'd expected taunting, but the silence was oppressive. But it was not as oppressive as the rank animal smell.

Most of the cells held two bunks, a small toilet, a shelf on either side, and a small one bar window in the back wall, set high above the toilet. Even with the bar removed, an average man couldn't fit through the window hole.

At the end of the walkway, there were two cells, one on either side, approximately three times the size of the other cells. The fronts were covered by poorly fitted sheets of metal, which effectively hid the interior. Deke unlocked one of the doors and swung it open. Heat poured out with a physical force.

"Sweatbox," Deke said. Unlocking and removing my wrist and leg manacles, he shoved me inside, slamming the door closed behind me.

I stumbled in the dark, falling to my knees.

Then I heard a chuckle and knew I wasn't alone.

A deep voice rumbled. "Mickey Cohen said to tell you hello."

ROUND FOURTEEN

I rolled myself to my feet and moved until I could feel a wall behind me.

My head was spinning. *Mickey Cohen...Mickey Cohen...It couldn't be.*

Slivers of light between the metal sheets placed over the cell bars were the only illumination. My eyes were adjusting, but not fast enough.

A heavy blow struck me in the chest.

Heat surged within me, and I heard whoever hit me howl in pain. It had been a strong sucker punch, but I'd barely felt it. I knew I'd been hit, but the blow should have crippled me.

A name surfaced in my brain...*Legba.*

I heard another set of feet shuffling toward me from my left. Instinctively, I pulled my elbows in and put my forearms up to cover my face. The punch, when it came, grazed across my defense, and I slid in toward my attacker.

There is a world of difference between boxing

and street fighting. I have been in both situations enough time to know the only way to survive is to beat *the flinch*.

One of our strongest human instincts is to flinch. It is the body's autonomic reaction to draw back or shrink from what is dangerous, to wince when pain is forced upon us. It is an instinct telling us to run. The flinch is a split-second when the body and brain freeze. Flinching guards you from the unexpected. It is one of the few instincts we are born with and never lose. It's why you throw your hands out when you fall. The flinch is what makes you pull back from danger.

But flinching in a fight can get you hurt or killed.

Fighters know all about the flinch. Successful fighters understand how to overcome it and use it to their advantage.

The *flinch instinct* was to curl up in a protective ball, to let the mention of Mickey Cohen's name stun me into inaction, to let the odds against me dictate the beating I was supposed to suffer. But the flinch and I know to each other well, and I've learned how to redirect *flinch instinct* into positive action—to use the flinch to *respond* in a situation instead of *reacting* to a situation.

Even before my second opponent could strike at me, I was moving toward him, effectively cutting down the power of his punch.

At its best, boxing is a gentleman's sport. That doesn't mean boxers are gentlemen, but at its purest, boxing follows a code of conduct. It is raised above simple brawling through the poetry of the human form. It is the elemental, stripped down, elegance of one man pitted against another. It's considered a sport, but nobody ever *plays* boxing.

Street fighting is survival. It is dirty, nasty, and one of the lowest forms of human endeavor, but I was good at it. As an MP, I hadn't survived the worst ports of call the Navy had to offer without being very, very good at street fighting. The danger was, I often reveled in it.

I held my forearms high and slammed them down onto the body I knew was in front of me. I felt a satisfying crunch of collar bone and heard a shriek of pain. I grabbed fabric and swung the man a hundred and eighty degrees, putting him between me and the first attacker. I slid my hands from the man's chest to his face, working by feel in the dark. While pushing him backward into the first man, I grabbed the back of his skull and gouged my thumbs into his eye sockets.

Through the confusion of battle, I kept pushing until the off-balance bodies in front of me hit the back wall. I then dropped my shoulder, driving it into the first man's chest. There was a rib shattering crunch and a guttural scream. Finally, I brought my knee up with a blast of power into his unprotected groin, trying to drive his balls into his throat.

The screaming stopped abruptly. The first body in front of me went limp. I stepped back, letting the body drop, then immediately crouched and drove my shoulder forward again into the other man, who had been pinned against the wall.

He grunted as the air was driven out of him. I pushed away, keeping my balance. He stumbled forward, unable to avoid tripping over the body on the cell floor in front of him. As he fell, I wrapped my left hand around my right fist and smashed downward with both arms. His head was where I'd blindly judged it to be. The power of my blow hit the back of his neck and sent his head straight down to bounce off the floor.

I was seething with adrenaline. Sweat poured off me in sheets. I felt more animal than man. I threw myself at the cell door. Bars on the inside, a sheet of metal on the outside.

I'd expected resistance, but it wasn't locked.

The door swung open on well-oiled hinges and I stumbled out. The bright lights of the walkway seemed intensified, and I was as blind as when I was thrown into the darkness of the sweatbox.

Something flat and hard crashed down on my back, pain shooting through me. I caught a glimpse of an axe handle. It was about to crash down again, but I had a split second to fight the *flinch*.

Fighters, boxers, get hit all the time. You get used to it. You know you have to go with the hit, ride it to rob it of as much power as possible. Our human instinct is to tighten up, but the result is deeper and more permanent damage. By not *flinching*—not tightening up and anticipating the blow—instead of crushing vertebrae, the second blow missed my neck and fell on the muscles across my shoulders. It hurt like hell, but I survived the blow.

The other key in a fight is making your opponent think you are more damaged than you are. You let your opponent judge you by their own standard, by how they think they would react if they had received the same punishment. You lull them until you are in a position to strike.

I lay flat and unmoving on the rough concrete floor of the cell block's walkway. My eyes were closed, but all my other senses were alert. The warmth I had been carrying in my chest was spreading through my body. It felt as if it were glowing across my back, dulling the pain where the axe handle blows had fallen.

I didn't know if I believed in voodoo, but I did

believe in whatever magic Mademoiselle Charlotte had thrust into me. I couldn't not believe. I could feel it flowing through me like the blood of lions.

"I think I *kilt* him," Deke's voice said on my left. He didn't sound remorseful.

From the angle of the first blow, I knew there must be a second man standing to my right. I kept my eyes closed listening, not moving. I let whatever or whoever was inside me work a spell of strength and healing. Mademoiselle Charlotte had proclaimed, *Legba will make you strong. Stronger than you are. Stronger than Kalfu.* Now was not the time to be a disbeliever.

A pair of boots shuffled, and I knew there was now somebody standing in front of me. "You better hope you didn't *kilt* him." It was Lucas Trask. "If you did, you'll be finding yourself in a grave next to him."

One of Trask's boots kicked my right shoulder none too gently.

I consciously let out a suppressed groan.

"Not *kilt* then," Trask said.

I heard him walk around me to the sweatbox cell door. I imagined him looking inside.

"This boy be some *kinda* tough bastard," he said. "Big Willy and Garth are cottonmouth mean and ape strong and they ain't moving. Probably don't even know what hit 'em."

"But I got 'im, boss. I got 'im." Deke was getting excited.

Lucas Trask chuckled. "If you say so, cousin. Now, pick him up and toss him in eighty-one.

Deke and Calvin Trask, who I could see through slit eyelids, dragged my dead weight down the walkway. I sagged heavily against Calvin while Deke unlocked the door to cell eight-one.

As soon as the cell door swung open, I peeled myself away from Calvin and stood outside the cell door next to him, grinning.

"Thanks for the lift," I said.

Both men were so shocked by my seemingly impossible recovery; they didn't move.

I looked over at Deke.

"I'll have to owe you the payback," I said. Then I walked confidently into the cell and, immediately stretched out on the too short sleeping platform mounted on one wall.

There was a silence of confusion; then the cell door clanged closed. I listened as Deke, Calvin, and Lucas Trask seemed to argue softly before walking away. There was a distant thunk of a heavy door as they exited the cell block.

There was a moment of silence; then a single hand clap rang out like a gunshot. Then another, and another. It was slow and measured. The slow clapping made its way down the cell block, past my cell, up and along the top tier of cells.

Three claps per prisoner, then the next prisoner with three more claps. It went on, and on. The sound made me realized there were no secrets in prison. The goons in the sweat room had been a welcoming committee. Even if they didn't know I was a cop, they knew I wasn't simply another hard time con. And if they knew, all the cons knew.

However, as I listed as to the hand claps rolling through the cell block, I understood these men had been waiting for me. Whatever I was outside of these walls didn't matter. Inside these walls, I was something else...I was *hope*.

The clapping returned to its point of origin and stopped. It hadn't been applause. It was the sound of rebellion.

Inside me, Legba was content.

ROUND FIFTEEN

I am not by nature a patient person, and I have suffered from minor claustrophobia since I was a child. Yet, as I lay in cell eighty-one on the wooden shelf substituting for a cot, I felt a perfect calm. A feeling of positive inevitability.

Not even thinking about how the goons had invoked the name of Mickey Cohen made a dent in my tranquility. It was all meant to be. Warmth filled my veins and flowed through my body, soothing all aches and bruises from the battering I had taken. The raging beast within me, which had escaped in the sweatbox, was quiet, yet alert. I could feel him there, a part of me. He wasn't all of me, but he was the savage parts; all of them forged invincibly together and waiting.

I could see things clearly in my mind. My worrying about being recognized due to my professional fighting career had been groundless. I had been the target right from the start. A trap had been laid with Marcus de Trod as convenient bait. Yet, there was also much more going on than it had first appeared when the photos of Marcus de Trod turned up in Chief Parker's mail.

Tombstone and I had always known New Orleans Assistant Superintendent Guy Banister's story barely held together. We had not questioned it because we were committed to following through with whatever game was in play. Despite his bluster and FBI background, Banister was as corrupt as the mobsters and dirty cops he was supposed to be prosecuting.

By aligning himself with Lucas Trask and his swamp family, Banister had picked a side in the power battle to control Louisiana organized crime. Voodoo induced or not, mob boss Carlos Marcello was in bad health and losing his grip. Lucas Trask was primed to take over. Banister was jumping ship to the winning side.

I remembered in his dealing with Crebbs, Trask had declared his ownership of the prostitute Crebbs was convicted of murdering. Trask obviously believed he was in a position to take over Marcello's crime territory. If Mickey Cohen had put Trask up to luring me in, he too must believe Trask was going to oust Marcello from power.

It wouldn't have been hard to bait the trap. For

most of us who claimed St. Vincent's as home, the lessons taught by Father Tim—in the ring and out—had stuck. Father Tim and St. Vincent's had given us the chance to make something of ourselves, a fighting chance in life. However, there were also those who lost the fight.

Orphans, by their very nature, grow up under dysfunctional circumstances. For every St. Vincent's success story, there were other stories of lives filled with tragedy, crime, brutality, and simple mistakes. Everywhere men are incarcerated, you'll find some who passed through the doors of institutions like St. Vincent's.

The tentacles of organized crime reached deep into every part of the nation. Mickey Cohen was a powerhouse on the west coast, but he paid allegiance to the east coast families and, through them, was connected to mob activities in the Midwest and the south. Using corruption and bribery, it wouldn't have been difficult to locate Marcus de Trod, or someone else from St. Vincent's, and have him transferred to the Sauvage. The tattooing in his armpits could just have been done more easily post mortem.

It was no stretch to see the connection between Mickey Cohen and Lucas Trask. Prohibition was a thing of the past, but there were huge profits to be made from large quantities of illegal alcohol, *white lightning*, which required neither taxes, import fees, nor declared income. An illegal distillery on the scale of what Trask had set up would be a gold mine. But like any other business, dependable distribution points were mandatory.

Mickey Cohen was a man who did not suffer setbacks lightly. After I'd taken out his fighter, Solomon Kane, in the ring, Cohen had completely lost his foothold in the fight game. It had not been the most profitable of Cohen's mob businesses, but having been a professional fighter himself, it was a favorite. Losing it had been a rough and publicly embarrassing pill for him to choke on.

If something caught in Mickey Cohen's throat, he was going to spit it out. Then stomp on it. He might not be able to take on the whole of the LAPD, but he had been able to target one particular detective—me.

If Mickey Cohen asked Trask for a favor to feed his psychotic need for revenge, to even the score for my destruction of his fighter Solomon Kane, Trask would have been happy to accommodate. It would have been an easy undertaking for Trask, buying him much goodwill and a solid friend in Cohen.

I wasn't sure how it was all supposed to play out, but I knew it wouldn't be pleasant. I also knew the feelings of positive inevitability I was experiencing had little to do with Cohen's plotting.

The week I'd been given to find out what happened to Marcus and to get the Adrieux brothers clear, was now a moot point. That week had been based on Trask not knowing who I really was or my true mission. The whole situation had been a set up from the start. I didn't have a week. I had a handful of hours. If I failed, I'd have forever.

I was counting on Tombstone's instinct for trouble. He seemed to know things in an investigation before anyone else. He was a step ahead when things turned ugly. This time a single step could mean the difference between death and survival. I hoped his skills were working overtime.

Back in Los Angeles, it would have been easy to scoff at the thoughts of voodoo and its supernatural trappings. Here, deep in the swamp, it was a different story. The rules were different. Here the veil between normal reality and mystical reality was very thin.

This was far bigger than a punk mobster's desire for revenge.

As every muscle in my body swelled with power, I felt the knowledge of another much more epic battle grow within me. When I had first seen Trask, I knew him for what he was. He knew me for what

I had become.

Soon, one of us would destroy the other.

***

A siren blared briefly, waking me from the comfortable trance into which I'd fallen. There was the sound of the cell block door opening and boot heels on the walkway. Cell doors were being unlocked, prisoners exiting to stand outside their bars. I saw a guard move purposely past my cell without looking in. I heard the cell door next to mine open and the guard call, "Get out here, Omar." A second later another cell door was opened down the line.

I stayed lying on my hard bunk with my arm propped behind my head. I saw the black arm of Omar, the man from the cell next to mine, slip between my bars and signal to me.

I was wary. Again, I wondered if these hardened cons actually knew I was a cop. If they did, it wouldn't matter to them that I was as much a prisoner as they were...or would it? I had heard the clapping make the rounds of the cells when I'd first been thrust into eighty-one. I had felt rebellion was as ripe as the heavy smell of caged men. Maybe a cop, determined to take Trask down, was what these men wanted and needed.

I slipped off my bunk and went to stand in the front corner of my cell, where the bars across the front met the wall separating me from the cell to my right. I knew Omar was standing out of sight, having pulled his arm back. I made sure not to get close enough for him to grab.

"Who you bring?" His whisper was low and guttural.

It was an odd question, but I heard the underlying superstition and knew the right answer. "Legba."

"We have been waiting for you," Omar said. "But Kalfu is strong." There was desperation in the whisper now.

I remembered what the channeled spirit of Mademoiselle Charlotte had said and found the right response. "I am stronger. Do what your heart has told you to do." My voice and my words were not my own. They came from inside.

"We are ready. The Trasks have held us down too long. We were told you would come. When you fight in the cage, the gates will be unlocked."

The voice of a guard rang loud. "File out!"

The cons outside their cells began to walk toward the exit to the cell block. Omar didn't look into my cell as he passed, but I heard him whisper one last sentence, "Keep fighting until the explosion." Then he was gone.

I returned to my bunk and reclined again. I was right about the prison being ripe for rebellion. Even caged men will only be treated as animals for so long. Tombstone had told me about the *swamp music*. It was the noises and sounds used from the outside to communicate with those on the inside. He had told me those inside who needed to know would be ready for me.

The prisoners were all murderous thugs. They had been sent to the Sauvage because they were the worst of the worst, or because Trask and his minions wanted men like the Adrieux brothers out of the way. But now these men had become a dangerous powder-keg. I was the spark.

I would be ready.

Legba would be ready.

ROUND SIXTEEN

Trask would come for me in his own time.

The wait was designed to drive up my anxiety. He wanted to make me *sweat*, to fatigue my mind with all the possibilities, real and imagined, of what might happen to me next. Torturers use the anxiety of waiting for pain to torment their victims, to prime them for the main event.

Cops knew about making suspects *sweat*. Leave a guilty suspect sitting in an interrogation room. Every minute seems like an hour. They can't stop thinking about their guilt. They become like a pump, primed to spill their guts.

However, I knew how to wait. If a boxer doesn't learn how to wait, he can leave his fight in the locker room, defeated before the bell for the first-round rings. No punches have been thrown, but the fight is lost.

It wasn't that I didn't get anxious. The body hates anxiety. So, under stress, the brain automatically releases chemicals to deal with the pressure. Those chemicals need physical activity to do their job. If there is no action, only waiting, then they turn sour, forming the gnawing feeling in the gut we call anxiety.

The body treats anxiety as an enemy. If restrained from either fight or flight, anxiety builds up and overloads the body's normal responses. Breathing becomes high and tight, cold sweat seeps out, thinking becomes cloudy. Anxiety can exhaust you physically and mentally. You have to recognize what is happening and find a way to positively channel the body's natural responses.

For me, anxiety becomes the scent of the chase, the taste of my enemy's blood, the pristine edge of a well-stropped straight razor poised to cut. I embrace anxiety as a lover. I was becoming still and deadly calm, internalizing every tantalizing drop of energy, building pressure, building pressure, storing it away, savoring it. Waiting, waiting, waiting—to explode.

When they finally came for me, there were four of them. It was Deke and Calvin holding axe handles and two others who couldn't be anything but branches on the Trask family tree.

"Put them manacles on 'im, Bo," Deke ordered, after opening my cell door.

Bo stepped inside, treating me like I was a snake about to strike. I stood up and he jumped back a foot.

"Get in there," the other guard shouted. He was a big boy whose once barrel chest had slipped down to his belly. He put a boot on Bo's backside and shoved.

"Stop it, Ferg," Bo yelped, staggering forward, eyes going wide.

I reached out and caught him as he came crashing into my arms. "Easy," I said quietly. "I'm not going to hurt you."

Bo pulled back sharply, relaxing only slightly when I held my hands out in front of me to let him snap the manacles around my wrists. There was a chain leash attached to the middle of the chain running between the manacles. Bo tugged on it tentatively, and I followed him out of the cell.

As I started following Bo down the walkway, Deke and the other guards moved in behind me. Deke took great pleasure in poking me in the back with his axe handle on every third step. He guffawed every time he did it.

I was beginning to feel like a baited bear.

At the end of the walkway, in front of the closed cell block exit door, stood the big man himself, Lucas Trask. His pose was straddle-legged, cavalry pants bloused perfectly over those shiny, knee-high, leather boots, black leather gloves on his hands. His long black hair fell back over his shoulders, the beads and leather *gris-gris* pouches around his neck seeming to writhe like intertwining snakes. I could feel evil emanating from him.

"You figure things out yet, boy?" Trask asked.

"You were expecting me."

Trask nodded. "You think I stay in control of this prison, of this swamp, of this state by not knowing who enters these walls?"

Inside, I could feel a throbbing beginning to feed off my pulse. My heart was pounding, yet it was not my heart. I was something more than I had ever been before.

"I didn't think you would come," Trask said. "Why would you risk your life for a man like de Trod?"

"Seemed like a good idea at the time."

Trask let loose with his high-pitched laugh. "And now?"

I shrugged. "Now, it seems everybody went to a lot of bother just to squash one cop," I said. "Guess Mickey Cohen wasn't man enough to take me on himself."

Trask stifled his chuckle. "East coast told Cohen to do things this way. Didn't want him dealing with the heat a cop killing would bring in Los Angeles." Trask gave me what I assumed was a smile, a predatory parting of the lips.

"So, you and Cohen are what? Trained lapdogs?"

Trasks' lips tightened again. "You do got a mouth on you, boy," he said. "I enjoyed beating de Trod to death to lure you here. Now, I will enjoy beating you to death."

"It's going to take a lot more than a bunch of in-bred, crackers to do the job," I said.

The words were barely past my lips before the ham hock of Trask's right fist lashed out at me.

I moved my head out of the way and shuffled to the right, pulling the leash chain out of Bo's hand. I moved again, ducking, knowing Deke would be making use of his axe handle.

Deke staggered off balance as the axe handle missed me and crashed into a concrete wall. His stumble put him directly in the path of Trask's follow up left. It was a looping roundhouse, landing squarely on the side of Deke's head. He fell like a logged tree.

Trask backed off, seeming to gather himself. I stood still, letting Bo grab up the chain leash hanging from my manacles. Trask looked down at Deke and then up at me. Calvin and Ferg were rooted in place.

I looked at Trask's left hand, remembering it only had three fingers and shouldn't have been able to deliver such a stunning punch. Trask saw me looking and opened his gloved palm to reveal the short length of metal dowel concealed within.

"I guess you're gonna need some softening up, you being a challenger for the light-heavyweight championship and all."

Trask's dead eyes held mine, and, for the first time, I felt the strength of the power within him. It was malevolent, unfeeling, deep and dark.

Recognition dawned. He was as filled with Kalfu as I was with Legba.

"I'm going to help you do what you came here to do," Trask said.

"How's that?" I asked.

"I listen to the *swamp music*."

"And what did it tell you?"

Trask sneered. "I grew up in these backwaters. I know every noise the swamp makes naturally, and every man-made noise of the *swamp music*. Charlotte Adrieux sent you to get her sons."

I gave Trask a questioning look. He stared right back.

"I've told them they can go free. All they have to do is beat you in the cage."

Trask cut his eyes to Bo.

271

"Bring him."

Outside, I could see the other prisoners from the cell block gathered on the benches around the cage in the middle of the compound. They were restive, looking around, talking in low voices. The uniformed guards surrounding them were on alert. Axe handles and shotguns were openly on display.

When I came into view, conversation stopped. Even the night sounds of the swamp became muted, like the volume of a radio being turned down. As Bo led me toward the benches and the cage beyond, a single hand clapped slowly. Two seconds later another hand joined in. Then another, and another. Gradually, all the cons began to clap together, slowly, deliberately, two seconds between each clap.

Bo led me to the path between the benches, and I got my first clear view of who was in the cage. The Adrieux brothers. They were twins; both built like Spanish moss-covered oaks. They were over seven feet tall, built sturdy through the torso leading up to the spread branches of their bare, black-skinned, heavily muscled, chests. Their hair was a wild profusion of matted and bushy curls. They were born and bred in the swamp, and it had made monsters out of them.

They both waited at the far side of the cage, wearing tattered boxing gloves, as I was marched up to the cage door opposite them. The barred door was opened by Omar, the black con who had been in the cell next to mine.

Before pushing me through, Bo unlocked my manacles. I still wore prison grays, high water pants, and an oversized shirt with the cuffs extending over my hands. On my feet were a pair of heavy, but comfortable boots.

The prisoners were beginning to whip themselves into a frenzy. Trask would use this spectacle, as he had all the previous ones, to diffuse the tension that built up in a prison setting. Men like these had to have an outlet for their violence. Trask didn't want their fury turned on his guards. By witnessing the cage boxing bouts, the inmates' blood lust could be cooled.

The bouts would help maintain discipline. Violations of the rules would not only lead to the sweatbox and beatings, but to the terror of facing the Adrieux brothers in the cage where there was nowhere to hide.

I turned my head and caught a glimpse of Trask stepping onto a backbench between a phalanx of his guards, every one of them *kin* to him.

I stepped into the cage. I felt Omar, who was holding the cage door open, press something into my hands. It was a pair of rough leather workman's gloves. I looked at him. He nodded and whispered, "Edmond is the slightly bigger twin," he said. "But Canray is the most dangerous."

I quickly slipped the gloves on my hands. Somebody had painstakingly sewn ridges of packed sand into the palms to provide extra punching power. They weren't quite as good as the *sap gloves* I'd worn when walking a beat, but they would have to do.

There was no preamble. The second the cage gate closed behind me, Edmond Adrieux let out a bellow and charged. I had a flash memory of the lion keeper in the circus cage I'd seen as a kid. He'd had a whip and a chair to fend off his charges. He'd even had a gun on his hip should the situation turn deadly. I had none of those things. But I did have my fists.

And I had Legba inside me.

I stopped Edmond with a straight right, staggering him when the blow hit him squarely in the forehead. There was a sharp *crack,* and the pain in my wrist was immediate and shattering, driving me to my knees. I had thrown the punch without thinking, without remembering the weakness I still felt in the wrist.

It felt as if I had shattered the bone. The pain was all-consuming. My entire arm was ablaze as if blood pumping through my veins was a raging fire. I was rolling on the ground in agony, but this didn't stop Canray from taking advantage of my weakness.

He reached down and grabbed the ragged front of my shirt and lifted me until my feet were off the ground. I could do nothing to stop his fist crashing into my face.

I had enough presence of mind to turn my head as the blow connected, but the power was stunning. There was a tearing sound as the material of my worn prison shirt shredded in Canray's hand.

I staggered back, my shirt in tatters around me. As Canray swung at me again, my only defense was to drop to one knee. His roundhouse passed over my head. I drove my left fist into his groin. He grunted and bent over. From my position below him, I launched a left uppercut into the point of his exposed chin. His head snapped back, eyes rolling up in his head.

A club-like fist smashed into the side of my head, and I rolled away. Edmond was back in the fight. The pain in my right arm felt as if I was burning from the inside out. My wrist was on fire, the pain so intense I was on the verge of passing out.

Edmond swung a clumsy roundhouse right. I instinctively threw up my right arm to deflect the punch. Sparks exploded behind my eyes as Edmond's punch made contact with my arm, but it was Edmond who reacted in pain as if he had been burned by the heat from inside me.

The fire in my right arm flowed into my torso, taking with it all the pain. There was a searing intensity centered in the small wound Charlotte Adrieux's fingernail had gouged in my chest. All the pain I'd ever experience in life was being sucked inside. There was a moment of numbness, and then a blast of energy flowed back out of the wound and through my body.

And the night exploded with noise and flame.

ROUND SEVENTEEN

The first sound was the roar of airboat engines as three of the flat-bottomed *swamp runners* raced toward the prison's dock. Within seconds there was a series of escalating explosions as bound sticks of dynamite were hurled into Trask's industrial distillery.

The noise of the explosions battered my ears with the force of a brutal punch. Outside the fighting cage, prisoners were running amok, charging into the prison guards surrounding the benches.

During the fight with the Adrieux twins, I'd been too preoccupied with pain to hear the yelling of the crowd outside the cage. Now there was a full-scale riot going on.

Flames shot up from the distillery along the end of the prison ground nearest the docks. There were more explosions as the fire ate hungrily into the flammable raw alcohol stored in large vats.

Edmond Adrieux was suddenly beside me. I

turned and was shocked to see him smiling. "Come! Come!" He gestured.

Canray still appeared to be disoriented. When Edmond grabbed one of his brother's arms, I grabbed the other, both of us leading him toward the cage entrance, which Omar swung open.

"Hurry," he said.

There was the sound of shooting and men screaming. Canray grunted and staggered, hit by several stray shotgun pellets.

The generator powering the three spotlights suddenly disgorged its innards as a stick of dynamite exploded on top of it. The glare of the spots instantly died, rendering me almost completely blind.

Then the night sky was illuminated by flares, and I spotted Tombstone on the bow of an airboat. He tossed the flare gun aside. Using the glowing stub of a cigar secured in his mouth, he lit the fuse to the strapped bundle of dynamite sticks. He tossed the bundle under the guard tower closest to him.

I swiveled my head, looking for Trask. I couldn't see him, but I could feel him. I could feel his anger.

And I could feel his fear.

Finally, cognizant, Edmond detached himself from my supporting arm. He reached over and grabbed Canray, who was slowing, and dragged him along as we headed toward the prison dock.

The biggest explosion yet ripped a gash in the night. It came from the front of the prison, where it blew out the crumbling cement block walls on either side of the main entrance. Without the support of the walls, the heavy steel entrance gates stood for a second then tipped inward, crashing to the ground. Two concussion-shocked prison guards were caught underneath the crushing weight. Dust and debris flew everywhere.

In the light of the now descending flares, I was relieved to see the green uniforms of US Army Rangers flooding through the gaping hole left by the fallen gate. Tombstone's Army connections ran deep, but he must have been owed a lot of favors to get the Rangers here.

Since the Sauvage Penitentiary was under federal jurisdiction, Banister would have been powerless to stop the Army from moving in. I had no doubt; he didn't even try. Banister would have reacted in an instant and scrambled to turn things to his advantage. Cockroaches always survived. Banister would be claiming credit for destroying Trask's corrupt organization before the night was through. Bringing in the Army would turn out to be his idea.

I had been disoriented by all the explosions, but with the impact of a striking fist, I was focused again. I could feel something rising inside me. It was something powerful, something ready for battle. My head snapped around searching for Lucas Trask.

Even with the light from the fizzling flares, there was too much commotion in the prison yard to be able to see anything other than jumbled silhouettes and shadows. There were more explosions as other vats within the distillery caught fire. Men battled around me. Shots were being fired.

I crouched and closed my eyes. I ignore the intensity of the noise around me. I took a lungful of air in through my nose, overloading my sense of smell with smoke and dust. I stopped feeling and let myself find my center as if I was about to step into the ring.

I felt energy flowing from my core, blazing down my legs into the ground beneath me. Energy flowed down my arms, out through my fingers, and into the surrounding night. I felt as if I was burning inside, my muscles being tempered like steel, my bones seared into an unbreakable skeleton. I felt as utterly and totally alive as I never had before.

And then I felt him. Felt Lucas Trask. Felt Kalfu.

The feeling came from the ground, in through my feet, and straight to my center. I open my eyes, stood tall, and turned toward the dock. I began to run. Ten steps later, I saw Trask raising his Winchester to his shoulder. He was beginning to take aim at Tombstone, who was jumping from the front of his airboat onto the prison's wooden dock.

Without thinking, I scooped a fist-sized chunk of concrete debris from the ground, hurling it like a fastball pitcher trying to get the last out in the World Series.

It took a split second for the projectile to cover the remaining distance to Trask and smash into his shoulder. The Winchester fired, but the shot flew past Tombstone to strike the man who had been in the driver's seat of Tombstone's airboat. The man cried out and fell to the deck.

Trask didn't hesitate. He bounded toward Tombstone and whipped the Winchester around like a club. Throwing up an arm, Tombstone deflected the brunt of the blow but was still bludgeoned backward.

I was running forward in pursuit, but Trask kicked viciously at Tombstone, knocking him first to one knee and then off the edge of the dock. Trask jumped onto the airboat. It was still running, and he grabbed for the controls.

I reached the dock, going down on my belly and reaching over the edge. I flailed blindly with my right arm but was immediately rewarded as

Tombstone's hand wrapped around my wrist. I half pulled, half dragged him back onto the dock.

Lying on the rough wood boards, we looked at each other and grinned. "You're early," I said.

"You complaining? You'd rather I'd waited the full week?"

"You've been busy."

"I got Banister alone. It didn't take much to convince him to talk straight or have the Army take him down along with Trask."

Trask...

There was a roar, and we were showered with swamp water as Trask accelerated away in the airboat.

Tombstone got rapidly to his feet, dancing around and shaking himself. Two long, skinny, shapes fell away from him and hit the deck. I jumped back. The shapes were cottonmouth snakes thrown up in the swamp water shower from the airboat.

Nothing was more important right then than kicking the snakes off the dock and checking each other to make sure there weren't any hidden hangers-on.

Two of the prison's airboats had fired their engines into life and slid to the dock next to us.

"You done jigging around?" Edmond asked from the pilot seat of the first boat. Canray was driving the second boat. I scooted onto the deck of the first boat. Edmond hit the throttle even before I could get settled. I looked back to see Tombstone hitching a ride with Canray.

Behind us, in the light from the still burning distillery, I saw the Rangers rounding up both prisoners and guards.

"Ain't going back behind no walls," Edmond yelled at me over the roar of the giant engine driven propeller behind him. A grin split the slab of his face in what I thought was amusement but could just have easily been spite. When this night was finally over, he and Canray would disappear into the swamp, which was fine with me. The Army and the New Orleans political machine would be busy with the remaining violent prisoners and corrupt guards. Two missing brothers, sent to the Sauvage through the manipulation of one crime family battling another, were not going to be a priority.

But the night wasn't over yet. The inevitability of the coming confrontation with Trask throbbing through me. I hungered for it.

Legba would not be denied.

ROUND EIGHTEEN

There was a battery-powered spotlight on the front of the boat. I scrabbled my way over and turned it on, but its light did little to penetrate the darkness of the swamp. I looked behind and saw the light from Tombstone and Canray's boat twenty yards back.

My heart raced as tall gum trees or hidden stumps appeared in front of us, seeming too close to miss. Edmund, however, handled the boat with the calm assurance of someone who had grown up in the swamp knowing it's every hidden hazard.

"We have to catch Trask," I yelled back toward Edmond.

He looked at me. I thought he nodded, but I couldn't be sure.

"Edmond," I said. This time my voice was not my own. I hadn't yelled, but the name came out loud and clear. I saw the expression on Edmond's face change, the white of his eyes growing huge in the darkness.

He pointed ahead.

There was no way to hear the sound of another boat over the roar of our own. But as I looked where Edmond indicated, I saw several pinpoints of light weaving through the swamp toward us.

Slowing slightly, Edmund spun the airboat around a trio of gum trees. Several more pinpoints of light winked on ahead of us. Two more appeared off to our left, and I realized the lights were from other boats all working in concert. Tombstone hadn't relied just on the Rangers to save the day. The Adrieux clan were out in force.

As Edmond maneuvered our boat. Canray and Tombstone's airboat moved up on our starboard side. We watched as the other boats moved in a herding motion, which became a noose tightening around the airboat steered by Lucas Trask.

Edmund feathered the throttle, skipping the airboat's flat bottom over a barrier of roots, pushing its prow through a wall of tall sawgrass and into a placid lagoon. He cut the engine, and we immediately slowed to a wallowing stop.

The lagoon was a hundred yards wide and formed a moat around a bare hump of land in its center. Tall and twisted gum trees grew out of the wall of tall sawgrass surrounding the lagoon. All around the edge of the sawgrass, swamp boats had settled, pointing the lights from their prows toward the center island. The boats were manned by shadowy men, swamp rats of the first order. Here and there flaming torches were set alight, both illuminating the area and infusing it with flickering shadows.

Fixed in the bobbing beams of the headlamps, herded to the location like a wooly mammoth pursued by cavemen, was the airboat piloted by Lucas Trask. The big man himself stood defiantly, legs spread, on the boat's deck.

<You bring my sons back to me?> The French words were said in the inimitable style and accent of Charlotte Adrieux, and my eyes were instantly drawn to where she stood in the prow of the boat nearest Trask's.

I felt myself standing, then almost physically being pulled forward. The boat beneath my feet began gliding ever so slowly toward the small island in the middle of the lagoon. The flat plateau gradually rose out of the swamp. It was circular in shape, about twenty feet in diameter.

"Your sons are here," I said, my voice low, but carrying across the water.

"Your sons are dead men walking." This came from Trask. He stepped from his boat onto the island and held up two of the leather pouches he'd been wearing around his neck. "I have their souls in my *gris-gris* bags."

I didn't need to look back at Edmond to feel the change in him when Trask held up the voodoo instruments. The airboat I was on gently eased onto the sandy incline of the island.

Other boats floated toward the island. Nobody got out of their boats, but they did reach out and sink the long poles of a dozen flaming torches into the soft ground. Charlotte Adrieux stayed standing proud and firm at the front of a swamp skiff polled by two tall, but rail thin black men.

Spreading her arms wide, she spoke in English. "Adrieuxs were part of this swamp long before Trasks arrived. The swamp flows through the blood in our veins. Your *gris-gris* cannot contain the soul of the swamp."

Trask let loose with his high-pitched laugh, spinning slowly around and around. This time nobody answered his laughter. When he was facing Charlotte Adrieux again, he feinted toward her, but she did not flinch.

"It is not my *gris-gris*. It is Kalfu's and Kalfu cannot be defeated."

"But you can," I said, stepping from the airboat onto the wet earth of the tiny island plateau.

Trask whirled to look at me, his face nothing more than a triumph of madness and evil. "You dare face Kalfu?" Trask gnashed his sharp pointed teeth at me.

I was angry and tired. Not physically tired. Physically, I felt incredibly strong and aware. But emotionally tired. I was tired of the game, tired of the voodoo, tired of bad men thinking they could steamroller everyone and everything.

I was angry about being manipulated. I was angry about what had been done to Marcus de Trod. I was angry about every fight I'd ever been forced to fight, and about every battle from the orphanage, through the Navy, and the streets of Los Angeles, in which uncaring wolves ravaged the weak.

I was not weak. With or without the power of Legba, or whatever it was within me, I was Patrick *Felony* Flynn, *The Giant Killer.*

Without warning, I sunk my fist with brutal force straight into the maw of Trask's mouth. He staggered backward, blood swelling over his lips, anger instantly replacing the shock flashing across his features.

Tombstone would later say what happened next was either a trick of the light or of the swamp itself, for Trask appeared to swell in size—both height and width. All I knew was I felt myself also swelling with stature and power.

Trask jabbed his huge right fist at me, but I brushed it aside, ready for his follow-up left. I had stripped off the remaining tatters of my shirt while on the airboat, but I was wearing the work gloves with the sand pouches sewn along the fingers. Trask had on his black leather gloves, and I was aware of the rolled lead concealed in the palms of his fists.

The dirt of the swamp mound was springy as a ring canvas beneath my feet. I shuffled across it easily, making Trask come after me like a bull chasing a matador. He swung at me again and again, heavy clouting blows I fended off with my forearms.

I was forced back to the edge of the plateau. I placed one boot-shod foot into the water, ducked under Trask's thunderous roundhouse right and drove a hard-straight right of my own into his exposed side.

I moved forward, out of the water, and felt something trailing behind me. I looked down and saw a cottonmouth had attached itself to my boot heel. Any higher and it would have latched on to my bare leg. The water surrounding the small island plateau must be infested with the deadly snakes.

The snake scared me more than Trask, and I jumped around like a voodoo-infused zombie. I finally swung my foot with enough force to dislodge the snake and send it spinning back into the swamp. In my dance of craziness, I lost focus on Trask, giving him the opportunity to blindside me. A crushing blow struck the left side of my head, and I spun directly into a hard left uppercut.

My hands dropped. I was barely aware of Trask stepping forward, his forehead snapping in toward my face in a head-butt. Street fighting instinct was all that saved me. I moved my head to the side and, as the force of Trask's body followed through with the missed head-butt, I brought a knee viciously up into his exposed gut.

He howled and staggered away. I wasn't in any better shape. Trask's blow to my head had unfocused my eyes. I staggered away in the opposite direction to regain my bearings.

On this island arena, there were no neutral corners, no referee, nobody to ring the bell to end a round. There was nothing outside the brutal ballet of this fight we both had chosen. Two men, *but only one winner.*

As my head cleared, I heard the sounds of strange chanting. It was coming from the boatmen. Above their constant sound was a higher wailing coming from Charlotte Adrieux. From the prow of her skiff, she stood with her hands weaving strange and complex motions.

The water around the edges of the island began to agitate as if it were boiling. The roiling of the water surged, and a tangle of snake-like coils became visible, tumbling to the call of Charlotte Adrieux's voice and the motion of her hands.

Trask loomed in front of me, impossibly large and solid. I dropped into a crouch and took the brunt of two crashing blows across my shoulders. I began to piston my arms, moving forward and forward again, driving a left jab, then a right, then a left, over and over.

I was impervious to the blows crashing down on me from above. I knew only one thing—I had to punch my way through the man mountain in front of me.

Slowly the wall of Trask's trunk began to crumble under my relentless onslaught. Here in the swamp, as in the ring, a man is only as strong as the core of his body. Chop down the core and the tree of the man, no matter how big, falls.

I punched again, and again/ My mind was lost in the hours and hours Pop Hawks had kept me striking the heavy bag, always pushing me to punch one more time, two more times, ten more times...

Pops made me into a machine—a machine capable of ignoring the fierce burning in my shoulders and the electrifying shocks moving through my arms. A machine drawing strength from every muscle in the body, feet, legs, and hips sending their energy forward into the relentlessly punching fists.

Trask gave ground.

His feet shuffled back, not of his own volition, but because his body could take no more. He was still swinging, but the power of his punches was fading.

I came out of my crouch and saw I'd battered Trask across the plateau. The water that had been at my ankles was now at his, the edges of it a churning foam. I threw a hard jab once more to his gullet but followed it this time with a lightning jab to his exposed throat.

He *urked* as his Adam's apple swelled to cut off his breathing. My next blow smashed his nose flat. Trask threw up his hands. He opened his mouth, and a harsh wind blew out of him, wrapped around me, twisted away and fled into the dark.

I delivered the final blow, a right cross thrown with every last volt of energy within me. As the punch connected, I had one split second to realize my right wrist was as solid as it had ever been. No pain. No hesitation. My punch was again the giant killer it had always been.

Trask's eyes rolled up in his head. I grabbed desperately to stop him from falling backward. But as I grasped for him, he slipped away and timbered into the roiling foam of water and snakes surrounded the plateau.

He was silent in his fall, and I watched in horror as his body was overcome and consumed by the hellish wriggling mass awaiting him. The black lengths of cottonmouths seemed to rush from around the island to the point where Trask was thrashing, each desperate to sink their fangs and draw the evil from him.

I became aware of Charlotte Adrieux's wailing, then a literal clap of thunder as she slapped her hands together over her head. In the sudden silence, the roiling of the snakes ceased, and the waters became calm.

In the flickering torchlight, the bloated and lifeless body of Lucas Trask floated facedown carried away by invisible currents until it was hidden in the sawgrass.

I felt myself drooping, but Tombstone was there beside me. His strong arms kept me on my feet.

"Archie Moore better look out for your right," he said.

EPILOGUE

The Army? You called out the Army!" Chief Parker didn't know whether to foam at the mouth in fury or laugh out loud.

"It was the best option at the time, sir," Tombstone said, straight-faced.

"And you, Flynn. You thought getting yourself sent to prison was a good idea?"

"You said to show 'em how we do it here, sir," I said. Throwing Parker's words back at him was a calculated risk.

We were in the chief's office the day after arriving back in Los Angeles; the journey taken by train this time. I ran the brim of my Fedora back and forth in my hands.

"And is that how we do things here?" Parker asked, his voice dangerously low.

"We do whatever it takes to get the job done, sir," I said, just as quietly.

Parker looked at me then cut his eyes to Tomb-

stone. "How did you handle this Banister character?"

"We didn't trust him from the start. With the
help of the Adrieux clan, I disappeared after the
fixed fight when Flynn supposedly killed the undercover cop, Danny Romani."

"Why?" Parker asked.

Tombstone shrugged. "Survival instinct. While
Flynn was around, I was safe. But with him incarcerated, I was just another expendable black man."

Parker nodded. "But there's more to the story?"

Tombstone shrugged. "The whole situation
smacked of bad *ju-ju*. When Flynn was set to be
transferred to the Sauvage, I had a quiet talk with
Banister to find out exactly what was going on."

"A quiet talk?"

"Yes. Just Banister and myself. I picked him up
at his house. Took him out through a back window
while his wife and a guest were sitting down to
dinner. Took him out into the swamp and intro-
duced him to a little voodoo of my own. It was
surprisingly easy to get him to spill his guts once I
provided a way for him to save face."

"And he is still running the anti-corruption unit
in New Orleans?"

"Taking all the credit for himself. According to
the New Orleans' papers, it was Banister's idea to

call in the Army, his idea to take down the corrupt Lucas Trask, and shut down the penitentiary."

Chief Parker shook his head. "Politicians," he said with disgust, as if he wasn't one himself. "And the other prisoners?"

I answered. "The Army rounded them up. They weeded out the ones who needed to be transferred to other federal incarceration facilities. They let the local jurisdictions deal with the prisoners who were there because Trask wanted them there."

Parker grunted. "This is all down to Mickey Cohen wanting to get revenge?"

"Yes, sir," I said.

Parker leveled his eyes to take in both Tombstone and myself. He smiled like a vicious bulldog. "Then no more running off on holiday jaunts. Mickey Cohen is a cancer in this city, and I want him cut out. Don't let me down."

We took our leave of his office. In the anteroom, Peggy Parsons, the chief's secretary, held out a note to me.

"What's this?" I asked.

"The chief had me making some calls while you were gone. He wants to rub salt into the wounds Mickey Cohen suffered when you knocked Solomon Kane out of the fight game. The championship shot supposed to go to Kane had to go to someone."

I looked at the name and telephone number on the paper Peggy had handed me. I held it up for Tombstone to see. His smile spread all the way across his face.

"Archie Moore's manager and his number," Tombstone said.

Peggy smiled too. "The chief thinks there will be no trouble setting up the fight card."

I rotated my strong right wrist. I felt inside me for the heat still there behind the spot where Charlotte Adrieux's fingertip had cut me. I was Patrick *Felony* Flynn, the giant killer, and I was getting my championship shot...

III. THE CHICAGO PUNCH:
A SHORT STORY

My name is Nick DeLuca. I write the Nightbeat column for the Chicago Globe. Stories start in many different ways. This one started with a punch from years ago and ended with a killer kayoed by a pugilistic priest.

In my youth, I'd thought I was pretty good with my dukes. That is until I was kayoed in the first round of the Golden Gloves competition by 'Tornado' Tim Brophy. My days of pushing leather dwindled by the time I was looking back at my teens. Instead, I'd started punching my battered Underwood with the sticking E key.

Still, I've never forgotten facing off against 'Tornado' Tim, especially as he went on to win the tournament. Over the years, we've remained friends. 'Tornado' Tim Brophy is now Father Tim Brophy, the battling priest. He's the heart of St. Vincent's Asylum For Boys, a local Catholic orphanage.

Father Tim, is beloved by the boys in his care. However, he is still a fiery personality and is constantly despaired of and prayed for by St. Vincent's nuns. He keeps his ruffian brood in-check by teaching every one of them the elements of the 'sweet science.' These are boys who come to him with no food in their bellies, no love in their hearts, and no hope for a future. Through boxing, Father Tim fills all those holes, turning boys into men in the process.

I walked into the East Street Diner just before the dinner rush and saw Father Tim waiting for me in a booth. There was a large woman in a loud, red-checked, jacket sitting next to him. Even from the door, I could see her size wasn't all fat. There was a lot of muscle on her bones as well. I pegged my hat on the stand and walked to join them.

"Nick! How are you?" Father Tim asked, standing to shake my hand. He slapped me roughly on the back with only a little less force than he'd used to put my lights out in the ring.

"A little bleary-eyed, Father. It's still a little early in the day for me."

"I wouldn't have called if it wasn't important," Father Tim said, sliding back into the booth next to his companion. I took occupation of the bench seat across from them.

A waitress with Iris on her name tag and stains on her white uniform sauntered over.

"Coffee." She didn't say the word as a question.

"Thanks."

She poured steaming liquid into a chipped porcelain mug, put it down in front of me, and walked away.

"Swank joint," I said.

"Your stomach is safe as long as you don't order the eggs." This came from the woman sitting next to the padre. "Bertha Levine," she said, introducing herself.

"Big Bertha Levine?" I asked. "The fight manager?"

"In the flesh," she said. "I should know, there's enough of it to go around." She laughed, making her double chins wobble.

I gave her a smile I'd been keeping in my wallet for just such occasions. It was a little worn. A woman fight manager was a rarity, but I knew Big Bertha had inherited her position from her father and her grandfather before him. It was in the blood as they say.

"You aren't looking for a rematch, are you, Father?" I asked, switching my attention to him.

The priest's eyes twinkled. "Now, there's a thought." He looked at Bertha. "Do you think we'd get enough customers to pay to see a reporter land on his keister?"

"I'd buy a ticket," Big Bertha said. "Never come across a reporter yet who didn't put more fiction than fact in a fight story."

I put up a hand to stop the friendly abuse. "I write the Nightbeat column, human interest stuff, not sports."

"I thought sports was human interest," Bertha said.

"Maybe, if it's got the right angle," I said. "You have a story for me?"

"More like a favor," Father Tim said. "Would you talk to an alumni of St. Vincent's who might be in trouble?"

"It's Felix Stokes," Bertha said before I could ask. "He's a middleweight. I had him on track for a title shot. Was starting him slow – making sure he got the right fights, so he didn't turn into a tin can palooka. Sweetest left hook, I've ever seen."

When I raised my eyebrows, Father Tim chimed in. "I know what you're thinking, Nick. Every fight trainer thinks his prospect is a contender, but I'm telling you, Bertha is right."

"What makes Felix different?"

"He's got the Chicago punch," Father Tim said.

I'd heard the term before. "You mean he's got heart …"

Father Tim nodded. "Not the one pumping in his chest, but the one that makes a fighter take every punch, get off the canvas every time he's knocked down and makes him the last man standing when the final round is over – that's the Chicago Punch."

"Very poetic, Father. Maybe you should be writing my column."

Bertha gave me a thunderous look. "You reporters are more cynical than a bookie on a losing streak."

"I've had a lot of boys come through St. Vincent's." Father Tim said, his voice reasonable, but firm. "My job is to turn them from lost orphans into decent men. I put 'em all in the ring to toughen 'em up, give 'em some confidence, and teach 'em the discipline to stay out of trouble and get ahead in life. Most of 'em never get in the ring again, but they carry what they learned with them forever. There's also been a handful talented enough to earn a living with their fists, but only one or two with the Chicago Punch, the heart to challenge for a title."

"And Felix is one?"

"Like none of the others."

"So, what's the problem?"

I looked at Bertha. She appeared almost reluctant to spill. After a moment, she spat it out.

"This ain't no sour grapes, you hear me?"

"Just tell it."

"Father Tim sent Felix to me to manage. He is something special – not just a good fighter, but a good man. His heart doesn't just fill the ring; it expands into everything he does. There isn't anyone Felix wouldn't help when they're down."

"You putting him up for a civic award?"

Bertha ignored my crack and plowed on. "Two weeks ago, Felix left me without an explanation. Went over to another promoter – Marty Deakins."

That rocked me back on my heels. Everyone knew Marty Deakins was connected. He had a reputation for dirty dealings second only to the mayor.

"Why?"

"Don't 'ya think I asked him that a hundred times," said Bertha. "He won't say nothing. Deakins has got something on him. It's the only explanation – otherwise, The kid wouldn't play it this way. I know him."

"The kid a gambler? Is that how Deakins got his hooks in?"

Father Tim shook his head. "Felix is a good kid – doesn't drink, doesn't gamble …"

"Women?"

Father Tim shook his head again. "Too shy and naïve – told me once if he couldn't be a fighter, he'd want to be a priest or, God save him, a writer."

Bertha had anger written all over her face. "Next Friday, Deakins is putting Felix in the ring against Silas Payne. Felix is going to get his head torn off."

"I thought you said Felix was the golden boy."

"He will be if he's handled right. Payne is little more than one of Deakins' trained gorillas, but he's got way more experience. The fight could ruin Felix."

"Why would Deakins snatch Felix away just to smash him?"

"None of it makes sense. It's why we want you to talk with him."

I shrugged. "Why do you think he'll talk to me?"

Father Tim answered, "Because he thinks you're aces. He reads Nightbeat every day. Loves the stories you tell. He admires what you write and what you stand for."

I felt a bit embarrassed. "All those words in the morning edition are lining birdcages by the afternoon."

"Not where Felix is concerned. He cuts them out and pastes them in a book."

"Where can I find this rabid fan?"

"Deakins trains over at Ten Count Gym. If Felix

isn't there, he has a room over Hillman's Bakery. He helps with the morning baking."

"Boxer, baker, candlestick maker ..." I sighed. "I won't promise anything, but I'll give it a shot."

***

I deal in putting words on paper, but there are many other ways of communicating. Boxing is one of them. It's a tough racket, but peel away the sweat and the blood and the bruises and you experience the basic language of men. Black men, white men, brown men, oriental, Jewish, Catholic, agnostic, Italian, Irish, Polish, Puerto Rican, illiterate, scholar, beggar man, thief – none of those things matter in the ring. The language of boxing is spoken with gloves pounding into muscle. The argument rages loudly until one man's arm is raised in victory.

Men in the ring speak to each other in ways only they can understand. It is a brutal telepathy of aggression punctuated with a Morse code of blows. The game can eat up young men like Felix, addle their brains and break their bodies. But true fighters, those who have what Father Tim called The Chicago Punch, or the New Orleans Punch, or The Anywhere Else Punch – will never stop expressing themselves. The ring is their paper, their bodies their pens. Fighters will always write their stories with the ink of pain and determination.

I drove to the offices of The Globe, catching the paper's boxing scribe Stan Kaplan at his desk. Stan was an old timer back when I joined the paper. Now, he was as ancient as the office furniture, but he knew more about the fight game than anyone else in the city – and he could still put a deadly string of words together.

"What are you doin' out before dark, scribbler?" Stan asked when he saw me.

"Reminding myself how dirty this city looks with the sun beating down. Tell me about a fighter named Felix Stokes?"

Stan gave me a look. "You know something I don't?"

"Probably – just not about boxing."

"Wiseguy." Stan leaned forward and started rifling through the mountain of papers and clippings on his desk. "Here it is," he said, handing me a clipping that ran to ten column inches of print framing two photos. The larger photo was of Felix in a traditional boxer stance. He was a good-looking kid with densely packed muscles. The second photo was of a woman whose facial features showed she was clearly related to Felix. From the style of her clothing, the photo had been taken a number of years ago.

"That's a piece I did on him six months ago."

"Who's the woman?"

"His mother. He was abandoned by her at St. Vincent's when he was six with a note saying she couldn't take care of him no more. Apparently, she put the photo in with the note."

"Sad story."

"It gets worse. Felix was adopted two days before Christmas when he was eight, but driving away from the orphanage with his new parents there was an awful car crash due to ice on the road. Felix was the only one to survive. He was only two blocks away from St. Vincent's before he had to go back."

Apparently, the kid hadn't gotten many breaks in life. "What kind of fighter is he?"

"He's was a comer."

"Was?"

"His new manager has him matched up against a goon next Friday. The safe money says Payne will take Felix apart."

"Is there a lot of dough riding on the outcome?"

Stan shrugged. "From what I hear there's a little more than normal, but nothing to write your Aunt Mary about."

"Any idea why Felix switched from Big Bertha to Marty Deakins?"

Stan shook his head. "It can't be on the up and up."

"What's the scoop on Deakins?"

"Rumor has it he's in deep with the bent nose crowd. He's scrambling to pay off debt, but his stable of fighters ain't enough of a draw to rescue him."

"Not even with Felix?"

"Felix is still fresh meat. If he'd stayed with Big Bertha, she would have brung him along slow, made sure he got the right fights at the right time. As it stands, he's got a small following, but he ain't gonna draw the kind of action Deakins needs – especially putting him up against a goon like Payne."

"And if Deakins doesn't come up with the scratch he owes?"

"Then he's gonna be trying to punch his way out of a cement overcoat."

"So, what's his play?"

Stan went silent and stared at me.

"What is it?" I asked.

"I heard something. Not even a rumor, just a whisper. Your kid could be in big trouble."

"Spill it, Stan."

"Some folks don't like their fights done up with gloves and Queensbury rules. They like a fight where only one man walks away. The whisper is Deakins runs a sideline in these death matches when he needs to raise cash. He brings the fancy in runs all the betting and takes home a large chunk of moola."

I knew the fancy was a fight term for the crowd that flocked to illegal bare-knuckle matches.

"You think Deakins is setting up Felix for one of these matches?"

"He has to do something to solve his cash flow problems."

"What about the fight with Silas Payne?"

Stan shook his head. "Not the kind of payoff Deakins needs. I'd say it's all for show, a carrot to get the kid hooked in."

"What's in it for the kid?"

"Maybe Felix didn't think Big Bertha was bringing him along fast enough." Stan shrugged. "Deakins probably promised the kid the moon but is playing him for a sucker. The kid is a scrapper. He might not draw a huge crowd for a legit fight, but in an illegal fight with a bad ending, Deakins could use the kid's freshness to pull in a huge crowd of heavy betting punters."

"You got any proof?"

Stan snorted. "If I did, I'd be spilling it across the Globe's front page – let my career go out in a blaze of glory instead of on the tale of another Friday night with two bums pummeling each other senseless." He turned back to his desk and pulled a

thin file out from a larger stack. "But I do have this
…" He opened the file and handed me the clippings
inside. "Two bodies were found a month apart last
year near the Union Stock Yards. Coroner put their
death down to misadventure – said they was hobos
who fell into the yards and got trampled."

"You think differently?" I said, glancing at the
clippings.

Stan shrugged. "Maybe. I only picked up on the
obits because both men, Olson and Cooper, were
over the hill fighters down on their luck. A body
that's been beat to death don't look much different
than one that's been trampled. Especially if there is
a payoff involved."

"Any connection to Deakins?"

"Both of them were set to fight Silas Payne the
week after they died."

I brought my eyes back up to stare at Stan. "What
are you trying to tell me?"

"To watch your back. I did some digging around.
Back before these guys turned up, Deakins was said
to be strapped for cash. Afterward, he was flush
and loud."

"But now it looks like he's in hock again," I said.

"Guys like Deakins always figure they're big and
tough and independent, but The Machine always
steamrollers them. Sooner or later, they're back

getting measured for that cement overcoat I mentioned."

"You ever get any answers to what really happened to these guys?"

"I'm a fight scribe, not a crime reporter. I passed the info on, but nobody was interested in the deaths of a couple of brain-damaged pugs."

"Can I keep these?" I asked, holding up the clippings.

"Sure," Stan said. "If it will help you save the kid."

He handed me the manila file folder and I stuffed the clippings inside.

I left Stan and walked to my desk. I poured a mug of Joe from the office pot on the way. It was a thick sludge, but I needed the caffeine. I lighted a cigarette to help kill the taste and sat down to read Stan's story on Felix. It was a heart warmer, designed to get the fight crowd behind Felix after Big Bertha had turned him pro. He'd won his first two fights and was setting up for his third when the article was written. Stan had done a good job of turning Felix into the kind of everyman hero fight fans loved.

It appeared, however, bad luck was still dogging the kid. There had to be some reason behind him turning his back on Big Bertha and throwing in with a pariah like Deakins, but there was no clue in the article. If I was going to unravel the mystery before Felix went down for the count against Payne, or maybe even worse, I figured I'd better go straight to the source.

***

The Ten Count Gym was an old burlesque queen dressed up in cheap finery, heavy make-up, and too much perfume. It was located in a rundown area on Pershing Road near Ashland. The rancid-sweet offal smell off the nearby stockyards was strong. The yards were right there, behind the strip of buildings that housed the gym, several sweatshops, and a string of dilapidated warehouses. The buildings had long been scheduled for demolition, but somehow they had avoided being torn down.

When I entered through the gym's battered front door, I was immediately assaulted by the stench of old sweat and older leather. There were three heavy bags hanging in a line to the left of the door. Two of them were weathering fighters' punches. On the right, two of the four speed bags were beating their rhythmic tattoo as men slick with exertion flashed flying fists against them again and again. I was surprised at how busy it all was for the early evening, but not everybody was a contender and had to work out when their day jobs were done.

The smells and noises of the gym were part of

the boxers' language. The yells of encouragement from the two dozen men outside the three rings in the middle of the gym were almost an inarticulate conversation of grunts and groans speaking roughly of desperate hope and chipped dreams.

In the two smaller rings, fighters and trainers were going through lackluster motions. All the real action was in the raised main ring where Felix Stokes was sparring with a brutish looking pug who sported a mashed nose and crew cut red hair. He had to be Irish.

One of the men spotted me. "Hey, you can't come in here. This is a closed session." Like most of the others, he looked like hired muscle, the kind who took care of business outside the squared circle.

"I'm just an interested member of the press," I said. "How's your boy shaping up?"

A tall, razor-thin man in a gray sharkskin suit, turned away from the ring action when he heard this exchange. He was clearly Marty Deakins. He had the face of a hungry ferret and a diamond stickpin in his tie.

When he moved toward me, I was surprised to see a woman standing behind him. She wore it well, but her dress was simple and ten years out of style. Like her dress, she was beyond the spring of her youth, but still shapely. She had a long fall of red hair framing an oval face. I felt I'd seen her somewhere before, but then I took in the black arches of her eyebrows and realized the packaging was hiding the true woman underneath. She was attractive, but there was a hardness around the edges of her eyes when she flashed them at me that spelled danger.

"I know you," Deakins said. His voice was a rasp as if he had trouble getting the words out of his throat. "You're DeLuca—from the Globe."

That picture next to my column sometimes closes as many doors as it opens.

"Guilty, your honor," I said, trying another smile on for size. This one didn't work any better than the one I'd tried on Big Bertha.

"What do you want?"

"I thought I'd do a story on your new prospect. I hear he's got a tough fight coming up next Friday."

"You ain't no fight scribe," Deakins said. "You're just a big nose butting in where you ain't wanted."

The two fighters in the ring had stopped circling each other, turning to see what the interruption was about.

"Hello, Felix," I said loudly.

Felix awkwardly removed his mouthpiece with a gloved hand. "Gee, Mr. DeLuca," he said. "Wow ..."

"Get back to work!" Deakins snapped. "You don't

talk to reporters before a fight."

Deakins brought his attention back to me. "This is a closed session. Either get out, or I'll have you put out."

I made the smart move and got out under my own steam.

I parked a half block down the street in the darkness under a broken street lamp. I could see the front door of the gym from where I sat. I patiently smoked a cigarette, cupping it in my hand to stop the glow from showing. It took the best part of two hours before I saw Felix leave the gym along with Deakins and his entourage.

I didn't want to approach Felix while he was still in reach of Marty Deakins, so I let him ride away on a beat up motorcycle that was only a small step up from an actual motorized bike.

Father Tim had told me Felix lived and worked at Hillman's Bakery, so I figured I could catch up with him later. First I wanted to see if I could get back into the gym. The lights were still on, and I figured there were still a few people inside, but with Deakins gone, I figured I'd chance my luck.

I left my car where it was and made my way on

foot around the back of the dilapidated edifice. Trash and debris abounded in the wide strip between the building and the low wall abutting the stockyards. I did my best to avoid puddles of unidentified muck to where the gym's fire door stood open. A stick of a black man with a towel over his shoulder was sweeping garbage out of the doorway. I knew him.

"Hello, Russell," I said.

The black man looked up at me. "Mister DeLuca. What you doing here?"

"My job, same as you."

"Last time we talked you were working over at Farrell's boot factory."

"That's my day job. Cleaning up here is my night job."

People like Russell were the heart blood of our city – working hard every day—and every night.

"How's your boy, Aaron, doing?"

Russell gave me a wide grin that was missing a few teeth. "Just great, Mister DeLuca."

"He still playing ball for Grambling State?"

"Yes, sir. Ever since you helped him get out of that trouble crowd he was running with, he been cracking the books and doin' what he s'pose to do. Me and his mother are still mighty grateful."

"Grateful enough to help me help out another

young kid?"

Russell gave a quick glance back over his shoulder. "What you need?"

"Five minutes in the locker room alone ..."

***

Russell let me in through the back door and then went back to the gym, leaving me alone. I checked along the row of battered lockers used by the gym patrons. The wooden cubbies were a freestanding row of simple cubicles with no doors. Four of them held battered training gloves, headgear, and sparing belts. Some of the cubbies were decorated with fight flyers, pictures of sweethearts, and other sentimental if worthless souvenirs.

I could tell which cubby belonged to Felix because the picture of his mother, the one reproduced in Stan's story, had been attached to one side. What was more interesting, however, was a newer photo. It was of the woman who had been standing behind Deakins.

I was right to think I recognized her. Stuck as it was next to the old photo of Felix's mother, it was easy to see the woman in the second photo as an older version of the one in the first. The fall of red hair surrounding the oval face had made the transition through the years untouched.

"I figured you'd be back!" A voice rumbled.

I turned my head to see Marty Deakins stepping into the locker room. He was followed by the fighter with the red crew cut with two other men on either side making a muscle sandwich.

"Get him, boys!" Deakins said.

I wasn't about to end up trampled in the stockyards. I snatched the two photos from Felix's cubby before reaching up to pull as hard as I could on the free-standing cubicle structure. It toppled down between me and the muscle, giving me the time I needed to escape out the fire door.

***

I made it to my car and sped away from the gym without being turned into a punching bag. I'd been sapped and clubbed and had guns pointed at me pursuing other stories, but it was never a highlight I wanted to repeat.

My Mercury was only a year old and almost found its way to the cop shop on Brussard by itself. I tipped my hat to the desk sergeant, who nodded me through to the stairs leading to the detective squad room.

Bill Reasoner was at his desk in the far corner.

He and his partner Mel Crider had been working the night shift so long their pallor was as white as the sheets on my bed.

"Quiet night?" I asked.

Reasoner took his feet off the lower drawer he'd pulled open in his desk and leaned forward in his chair. "Typical newshound, trying to tempt fate."

Crider walked over to join his partner. He was shaking his head. "Asking questions like that can set off a crime wave – you should be ashamed."

I shook hands with both men. They were tough guys, but they had to be. They did their job well, which was more than could be said of some who wore the same badge.

"You guys got anything on Marty Deakins?" The two bulls looked at each other. Crider answered. "He runs a string of thugs he calls boxers."

"He's not big time yet, but he wants to be," Reasoner chipped in.

"You ask me," Crider said, "He's trying too hard. I hear he owes the boys who run The Machine a little too much juice to play with them on the level. He wants to be independent, but can keep on the right side of the bookies."

"Few can," I said.

"A mug's game," Crider agreed, somehow keeping a straight face despite the Racing Times on his desk.

I took out one of the photos I'd snatched from Felix's locker. "She look familiar to you?" I extended it toward the detectives.

Crider took a long squint before handing it to Reasoner, who put on a pair of reading glasses before looking at the snap.

While Reasoner was pondering, Crider walked over to a wall cabinet and pulled out a drawer. He walked back with a file, which he opened and rifled through. "What do you think?" he asked Reasoner, taking a mug shot out of the file and handing it across.

Reasoner did a comparison and then turned both the snap I'd given him and the mug shot toward me.

"It's the eyebrows," I said after a moment. "Who is she?"

"Deakins sister, Hester," Crider said. "Did a stretch for check kiting. Got out a couple of months ago and made a beeline back to her brother."

I took the two pictures from Reasoner. In the mug shot, Hester Deakins had short cropped bottle-blond hair, but the dark arching eyebrows were the same as the redhead in the other picture – the woman I'd seen standing behind Deakins.

I now had the start of an idea of how Deakins lured Felix Stokes away from Big Bertha. It was amazing what you could do with wigs today.

The squad room phone rang. Crider snatched it up. He grunted into the receiver a few times, penciling notes on a pad, before hanging up.

"Uniforms in a prowl car broke up a beating down by the stockyards. Perps got away, but the victim is still breathing – male, black, named Russell Brown. The ambulance is taking him to City General." Crider turned his attention to me. "Better tag along scribe. The victim is asking for you."

***

I followed Crider and Reasoner's black detective sedan as it sped to the hospital emergency room. All the way, I felt sick to my stomach. Deakins and his boys must have turned on Russell after I'd made my escape. I felt more than a little responsible.

At the hospital, the doctor was not happy when Crider and Reasoner insisted on letting me talk to Russell. Apparently, however, the beating, while serious, had not been life-threatening. The uniform boys in the prowl car had stopped things before they'd gone too far.

"They was gonna throw me in the stockyard. Let me be trampled by the cows." Russell told me through his swollen mouth. He had a number of cracked ribs, a broken arm, and a multitude of contusions. "Them blue-suiters turned up before they could throw me over." Russell tried a broken tooth smile. "First time I ever been glad to see flatfoots."

"They say you won't tell them who did this."

Russell shook his head slowly. "Not my way. Makes too much trouble for people like me. I gots to get out of here and take care of my family.

"You just worry about getting healed. Did Deakins and his boys do this because they the thought you let me in?"

Russell slowly shook his head again, his black eyes turning purple from the beating. "No, sir. They didn't know. They caught me listening in on what they was saying about grabbing Mister Felix and making him fight tonight."

"Tonight?"

"Mr. Deakins said you wouldn't stop snooping, so they better set the match up tonight. He was just getting ready to send his boys to get Mr. Felix when they caught me."

"Do you know where this fight is supposed to be?" "Somewhere in the stockyards, but it ain't no fight ..."

"What are you talking about?"

"Mr. Deakins, he knows people will pay big money to see men beat each other with their bare knuckles."

"But why Felix?"

"Because he'll do whatever Mr. Deakins says to protect his momma."

I used the hospital payphone to call Father Tim. He spluttered and blustered when I told him my thought process, but he agreed to do what I asked him. When I explained what I wanted to Crider and Reasoner, they jumped on the bandwagon as well. You couldn't trust too many cops in this town, but I could trust them.

Back in my Mercury, I made good time through traffic to Hillman's Bakery. The storefront was closed, but there were lights on in the back where the baking was done.

I pounded on the bakery's back door until it was opened by a huge round man in a white apron and flour dust on his arms. He looked angry.

"What's the ruckus?" There were heavy traces of Germany in his accent. It didn't take a lot of brain power to figured he was Hillman, the baker.

"Mister Hillman, my name is Nick DeLuca. I'm with The Globe. It's important I talk to Felix McCann." I knew Felix was there because his low powered motorcycle was leaning against the back wall.

"Wow, Mr. DeLuca …" Felix had come up behind the baker.

Hillman scowled. "Make it quick," he said. "We've got bread to bake." He turned back into the bakery leaving Felix and me to talk.

"I read your column every day, Mr. DeLuca. It's great …"

"Thanks, Felix, but it's your boxing I want to talk to you about."

Even in the shadows, I could see Felix's face darken. "Is this about me leaving, Big Bertha?"

I held up the picture of His mother. The one left with the note when he was abandoned on the steps of St. Vincent's. "Your mother," I said. Felix grabbed the photo from my hand.

I then held up the other photo I'd taken from his gym cubical. In the other hand, I held up Hester Deakins' booking photo. "Not your mother," I said. "Deakins' sister … Hester."

This time Felix was slower to respond. He took a step forward to look more closely at both photos. I saw a tear start in one corner of his eye.

"I'm sorry, I said. "I didn't mean to be cruel, but I think you're in danger and I had to act fast."

Felix reached out and took the photo of Hester

Deakins in her red wig. "I thought she'd come back. Deakins told me she was in big money trouble and only if I did what he told me would she be safe."

"He tell you the only way to get the money she needed was to fight for him in a bare-knuckle bout?"

Felix swallowed. "How do …?"

"Now, isn't this nice," Deakins' voice made me turn around. He was flanked by his muscle boys, both of whom had guns in their mitts. The big Irish fighter with the red crew cut appeared in the doorway behind Felix.

There was nowhere to run this time.

***

Deakins and his goons hustled us away from the bakery in a well-oiled routine. They had snapped sets of handcuffs on both Felix and myself. They didn't have any trouble getting mine on, but three of them had to sit on Felix. Still, the deed was done without too much trouble.

I was just grateful they didn't plug me where we stood. I was banking on the fact they didn't want the kind of questions a reporter's corpse with a bullet causes to get asked.

Deakins, however, told me upfront my fate

wasn't going to be pleasant. "Won't be much left once we run your corpse through the meat grinder at the packing plant and slop the remains the hogs."

I was thinking on that image as the sedan the two goons stuffed me in sped away from the bakery. I could tell we were heading in the direction of Ten Count Gym and the stockyards. It wasn't much of a shock.

It was a tight squeeze in the sedan. I was pushed up against Felix on the backseat with a goon on either side. Deakins was in the front passenger seat with the Irish Pug, who Deakins called Silas, driving. So this was the vaunted Silas Payne. What had he been doing sparring with Felix earlier? It wasn't often opponents sparred the week before their bout. It seemed Deakins' fights were fixed in more ways than one.

"I'm sorry, Mister DeLuca," Felix said.

"It's okay, kid. You didn't know. Thugs like Deakins are just a blight on everything good in the world."

"Shut up, you," Deakins said, pointing his gat at me over the back of the front seat. "I'll happily plug you where you sit."

"I ain't doing nothing for you," Felix said to Deakins.

"Now, that's just too bad," Deakins said. "You see

I've offered some folks a good show, but they don't care if it's with a fighter who might just hold his own or a reporter who is just going to get beat to death."

"What do you mean?" Felix asked, not being as quick on the uptake as I thought he might be.

"You knew you were going to be going bare-knuckled and toe-to-toe with Silas here for the sake of your momma. Now you know your momma ain't your momma, you're still going to fight."

You're a rat," Felix bounced forward until one of the goons shoved him back against the seat. "If I didn't have these cuffs on ..."

"You'd what?" Deakins said and then snorted. "You do as I tell you and if you beat Silas maybe, just maybe, I don't feed your reporter friend through the meat grinder."

"He ain't gonna beat me," Silas said, his eyes flashing up into the rearview mirror. "I'm gonna crush him, Mister Deakins."

Relaxing slightly, Deakins put his gun out of sight. "Be sure you do, Silas, or you'll be fertilizer for the stockyards."

"What kind of crowd are you going to get on such short notice," I asked Deakins.

"These types of fights are always short notice.

That way the cops don't get a whiff of the action and try to spoil the fun."

"How does it all work?"

"You've got a big nose, don't you? Just like all reporters. You'll just have to figure it out."

"The way I figure it," I said, figuring I didn't have anything to lose by keeping Deakins talking, "You're never going to get out of hock to The Machine no matter how many of these illegal fights you stage."

"What do you know about it? Nothin', that's what."

"How many fighters like Olson and Cooper are you going to find?" That grabbed Deakins attention. Olson and Cooper were the two fighters whose obits Stan Kaplan had shown me. "How many more payoffs can you give to the coroner to say a dead hobo fell into the stockyards and was trampled?"

"Happens all the time," Deakins snapped at me. "Somebody is always trying to rustle stock when it's penned up. Makes a good meal for a lot of men down by the railroad camps."

"I think you're running out of options," I said. "When you're resorting to tricking or forcing men into these brutal fights for the prurient interest of the crowd, your plan is going to come apart at the seams."

Deakins shrugged. His voice was quieter. "Maybe, but not this time. Not in time to save you."

We'd see about that.

***

Another ten minutes of driving and we arrived in front of Ten Count Gym. From the number of cars parked in the area, Deakins' method of gathering his crowd on short notice was quite effective.

"How do you get the word out," I asked. "It can't just be word of mouth."

Deakins was too pleased with himself not to tell me when I asked this time. "Phone boiler room," he said. "Rotary lines. I've got the most modern set-up in town. I also use runners to get the word to those who don't have phones, but can't resist a wager."

"You must also charge admission."

"Not only admission, but a subscription to stay on the informed list." Deakins was as proud as a new papa. "But the real money is in the betting. I get a commission on every wager, and the house never loses. There's more than enough money to keep me independent and on top."

"Why not just fix the scheduled fight between Felix and Silas?"

"A news hack like you is never going to get

it right," Deakins said. "A regular fight fix has to have the approval of The Machine, and they get the largest cut. My special fights are mine alone. I don't share the takings with nobody."

I didn't say anything, but I knew that attitude would only last so long before The Machine mowed him down as they've done to every other criminal upstart in this town who didn't play ball.

Silas brought the car to a stop in front of the gym.

"Get out, "Deakins said. "You'll see what this is all about soon enough."

As we exited the car, I purposely tripped and fell against Felix.

"Just keep the fight going," I whispered urgently.

He looked at me in surprise. It was dark enough for me to risk giving him a quick wink and a nod.

We were hustled around the outside of the gym to a wooden gate in the low wall bordering the stockyards. I hadn't seen it when I'd been back in that area before. It led to a fenced corridor about six feet wide running between the stock pens.

In the dark, walking over the dirt of the uneven ground with my hands cuffed behind me was not easy. Lithe and athletic, Felix didn't appear to have as much trouble following Deakins and Silas. The two other goons were behind me bring up the rear.

After a hundred yards, the fenced corridor we were following led into an open pen. Trailer flatbeds had been wheeled into positions along the sides leaving a bare, muddy, patch in the middle, which I assumed would be the ring.

Atop the flatbeds, men from all walks of life, dressed up and down, were standing and talking loudly. They were all bound together by the lure of gambling and the visceral promise of men pounding each other with bare fists at the cost of their lives.

The smell of stock and manure was almost overpowering, The noise of the steers crammed together behind the wooden pens on the other side of the flatbed trailers was a constant cacophony. It was as if the beasts sensed not their impending doom, but the anticipation of the bloody event about to be wrought by the mass of humans now penned in the area themselves.

Eight tractors had been stationed between the trailers. Their engines were running and their headlights provided a ghostly illumination of the muddy arena.

The two goons pushed me up against a wooden fence gate. I could feel the heat and surge of the agitated steers, their lowing infiltrating the night with their plaintiff wails.

I felt behind me with my handcuffed hands, feeling for what I hoped would be there – and found it – a simple latch, no lock, but stuck firm.

Deakins led Silas and Felix into the center of the muddy flat.

"Are you ready, gents?" Deakins bawled in a carnival barker's voice to be heard. The roar of his gathered fancy answered him with barely restrained impatience.

Silas had stripped off his shirt, showing off a prodigious amount of muscle to the approving crowd. He flexed and threw a few shadow punches.

Deakins made a show of taking off Felix's handcuffs by shoving him into the muck on the ground first. With the unlocked cuffs in his hand, Deakins backed away. Felix stood up, his face a mask of bewilderment.

"All bets down?" Deakins asked loudly, looking to men standing on the corner of each flatbed trailer. Each one raised his hand in positive response.

The two goons with me were paying me scant attention. Like the crowd, they were caught up in the spectacle.

Silas suddenly stepped forward, delivering a bare-fisted right jab into an unprepared Felix's face. The younger, slighter built fighter dropped like a poleaxed bullock. He took two blows from

Silas' hobnailed boots before he found the instinct to move.

What happened next made me think Felix was not as stunned by all the action as he appeared. Instead of rolling away from Silas' boots, Felix rolled toward his opponent. As he flowed to his feet, he brought a fist up with him, driving it into Silas' unprotected groin. Apparently, Father Tim had taught his boys the 'unsweet science' of street fighting along with traditional boxing skills.

On his feet, with Silas doubled over in front of him, Felix flitted to the side, driving one fist and then the other into Silas' unprotected kidneys. Silas roared like a lion with a thorn in his paw, twisting to the side and whipping his long arms around to get at Felix who had danced away.

Felix was a smart fighter. He didn't waste time or put his hands at risk by hitting Silas in the face with clenched fists. Chances were he'd break a hand if he missed and hit Silas in the forehead or skull.

Refusing to stay in and trade punches, Felix took advantage of his speed to dart in and out, feinting with open-handed jabs at Silas' face and then shifting to deliver driving blows to Silas' exposed ribs or kidneys.

For his part, Silas was in a rage like a bear fighting a bee. He kept turning and turning, trying to keep up with the faster Felix, getting stung again and again and never getting to retaliate with a solid blow.

The crowd didn't like the action any more than Silas did. They yelled their disapproval and threw whatever they could lay their hands on at the two fighters. They wanted blood and murder.

Obviously worried about customer satisfaction, Deakins stepped in and took a hand. Wielding a discarded piece of fence post, Deakins stepped up behind Felix and struck him flush on the back, Felix staggered forward into Silas' grip all to the roar of approval from the crowd.

Silas didn't waste time once Felix was in his clutches. Holding the back of the stunned Felix's head, Silas drove two hard jabs into his victim's face. The wet smack of the punches as Felix's nose spewed blood brought the crowd to a frenzy.

I couldn't wait any longer for my first plan to come to fruition, so I improvised a backup plan. While the two goons with me had been watching the action, I'd been working and working at the gate latch behind my back.

Finally, it sprung loose, the surging of the packed beasts behind it swung the gate open as I jumped to the side and out of the way. The agitated steers flowed into the pen where the fight was being held.

One of them jumped onto a flatbed, scattering the crowd there down into the muck and swirl of the other animals.

Police sirens and whistles suddenly rent the night and blue uniformed men with truncheons and saps waded in, swinging without discrimination. I spotted Crider and Reasoner leading the charge. Crider saw me and stopped his enforcement action long enough to get the handcuffs off me.

"You took long enough to get here," I said. "I thought Father Tim was supposed to follow us from the bakery while you went for reinforcements."

"Quit complaining," Crider said. "We got here, didn't we. Father Tim couldn't find a working payphone in this area once he knew where you were headed."

"Where is he?"

"In front of the gym. Had a hell of a time making him stay out of the action."

As Crider turned back to join his partner, I rubbed my wrists and tried to find Felix in the confusion. The bovines had slowed from their first mad rush, but their huge bodies kept most of the crowd from moving off the relative safety of the flatbeds.

I finally spotted Felix. Apparently, even being blindsided with a fence post and repeatedly punched by his opponent couldn't keep him down. He had taken advantage of the confusion to slip from Silas' grip. Suddenly, with his hands wrapped around each other, he swung both arms in a devastating arc. The blow he delivered to Silas' jaw twisted the bigger fighter around, sending him to the ground with the looseness of unconsciousness – A kayo in anyone's book.

However, Felix wasn't done. He spotted Deakins edging away from the crowd and lit out after him. Somehow, Deakins had managed to escape the press of the animals and the perimeter of uniformed cops. He saw Felix running toward him and took off like a scared rabbit.

I ran after both of them, stumbling as I tried to avoid obstacles. I didn't want to have gone all through this only to have Felix end up on manslaughter charges or worse for taking his anger out on Deakins when he caught him.

I trailed behind them as they ran down the corridor we had used to enter the pen back toward the rear of the gym. I spat out of the corridor just in time to see a most welcome sight.

Father Tim hadn't waited in front of the gym. He was still too much a man of action to be kept back for long. Deakins was looking behind him, running in fear from Felix, when Father Tim stepped out of

the shadows and delivered the sweetest right cross
of his fighting and priestly careers.

As the blow struck, Deakins' face stopped, but
his legs kept going – running right out from under
him. He landed flat on his back in a puddle of muck
– down for the count.

**

It was almost breaking dawn by the time I got back
to my desk at the Globe and rolled the first sheet of
blank paper into my Underwood.

Crider, Reasoner, and their uniformed troops
had done a great job of rounding up the crowd,
taking names for later prosecutions and booking
those with known warrants. Silas and the two
goons were cooling their heels in the station holding cells. Deakins himself was under guard in the
hospital – getting his jaw wired.

Father Tim had brought Big Bertha with him,
and their reunion with Felix was bittersweet.

As for the kid himself, Felix had lost a lot growing up. He'd now lost his mother yet again – not
his real mother perhaps, but certainly, the hope of
family connections so many orphans carry with
them. But, the kid was a true fighter. He wouldn't
whine about it. Being a true fighter, he knew how

to channel his pain without ever asking, "Why me?" or blaming somebody else. If you got into the ring, you were bound to get hit, but you didn't have to go down – especially if, Like Felix Stokes, you had The Chicago Punch.

"Copy!"

A LOOK AT: Paul Bishop Presents... Pattern of Behavior: Ten Tales of Murder & Mayhem

EVERY STORY IS A GEM OF CRIME AND PUNISHMENT...

Bestselling author and crime fiction expert, Paul Bishop brings together ten tales of murder and mayhem from the devious imaginations of both top crime writers and the genre's rising stars.

Filled with unforeseen twists and turns, these tales range from dark to deadly, each one designed to snatch your breath away.

Includes Stories by Paul Bishop, Eric Beetner, Nicholas Cain, Ben Boulden, Brian Drake, Christine Matthews, L.J. Martin, Richard Prosch, Robert Randisi, and Nicole Nelson-Hicks.

AVAILABLE NOW

ABOUT THE AUTHOR

Novelist, screenwriter, and television personality, Paul Bishop is a nationally recognized behaviorist and deception detection expert. A 35-year veteran of the LAPD, his high profile Special Assault Units produced the top crime clearance rates in the city. Twice honored as LAPD's Detective of the Year, he currently conducts law enforcement training seminars across the country.

Paul is the author of fifteen novels and has written numerous scripts for episodic television and feature films. He starred as the lead interrogator and driving force behind the ABC TV reality show Take the Money and Run from producer Jerry Bruckheimer.

He regularly presents his popular seminar, Six-Gun Justice—Western Novels, Movies, and TV Shows, at libraries and other community functions.

Find Paul online:

www.paulbishopbooks.com